ENJOY ALL OF SOPHIA SUMMERS' BOOKS

JOIN HERE or at her website for all new release announcements, giveaways and the insider scoop of books on sale. http://www.sophiasummers.com

Her Billionaire Cowboys Series:

Her Billionaire Cowboy

Her Billionaire Protector

Her Billionaire in Hiding

Her Billionaire Christmas Secret

Her Billionaire to Remember

HER BILLIONAIRE CHRISTMAS SECRET

SOPHIA SUMMERS

CHAPTER 1

$\mathcal{T}$he snow fluttered down onto Peter's windshield, the flakes getting larger the longer he waited. He sat in his Jaguar, with the motor running, a few houses away from the Woodlock home. He watched until all the lights went out. As the flakes started to clump together, it looked like there might be a white Christmas in Kentucky this year. Their home was in an older, but well-kept, neighborhood. Large trees graced the small front yards. Each house was decorated with Christmas lights of every color, and the porches were adorned with garlands and red bows. But the Woodlock home stood out. Lights wrapped the whole house, not just the front porch, and the trees were glistening with bright color.

He waited an hour and then quietly opened the trunk and took out a bright red Mongoose 20-inch Outerlimit BMX bike. He rolled it over to their house and placed it on the front porch. The bike lock that he pulled from his pocket secured the bike to the porch railing. As he walked back down the sidewalk, he placed an envelope in their mailbox with the combination.

Peter drove off, another anonymous Christmas present for Dani and her son Sam delivered. He turned up the Christmas music on the radio and sang along. As he drove through the country-side to the airport, he thought back to the days when he'd been on the receiving end of the Dugan family's love. He had lived next door to them from the time he was four years old.

Whenever his father had too much to drink, his mother always said, "Dad is sick Peter, he needs his rest." But he knew from his schoolmates that his father was an alcoholic. His mother was so busy working to support the family that he rarely saw her, and when he did, she was too exhausted to speak with him. He remembered laying his head on her lap while she watched TV and slept in her ratty, old kick back chair. "Mom, I did well in school today." She would reach her hand down and pat his head and fall back asleep. These moments would have been the only comforting memories of his childhood if not for the Dugans.

The day they moved in next door to the Dugans, Danielle came over to watch his father carry furniture into the house. "What's your name, boy? I'm Dani." He smiled as he pictured that little Dani with hair so curly it was constantly escaping the pigtails she wore each day. The frizz created a halo around those rosy-red cheeks. Her deep green eyes sparkled with excitement, and her dark brown hair stayed sun-kissed all year long.

She stood on his front porch, all smiles and confidence. He was so shocked that she spoke to him he turned around and ran back into the house. She followed him inside and found him in an upstairs bedroom, sitting in the corner. She pulled a Tootsie Pop out of her pocket and gave it to him, then she unwrapped one for herself. "Come on, do you want to see our kitties?" He'd followed her, just like he had every day since. Dani became his best friend.

As he got older, he realized fully the shame of having a father who was the town drunk. Kids made fun of him at school. Peter still cringed as he remembered a day when the neighborhood kids were outside playing softball at the corner. Gary, the boy on second base, was making catcalls to Peter as he came up to bat. "He's a loser just like his Dad. We can strike him out." Peter hung his head in shame, trying not to cry. Then Dani ran up behind Peter, grabbed the bat, and took off after Gary. Gary tried to back up but not soon enough. Dani slammed the bat into his shins, and he fell over, crying.

"Dani, what's your problem?" Gary cried. The other kids who had been laughing, moved away from Dani, wary.

"Don't make fun of my friend!" Dani yelled. She marched back to the plate and gave him back the bat. "Okay, let's play now." He had been amazed.

As time passed, he spent more and more of his waking hours at the Dugans' home. He ate dinner there most days, and every day, Dani's mom, Mary, packed him a lunch. She often pushed his hair out of his eyes. "Peter, I swear, your hair is as curly as Dani's."

His mother worked two jobs and also did the darning and some simple alterations for the Dugan family. He knew his mother appreciated the meals and lunches they gave him while she was away at work. She would often say, "You mind your p's and q's at the Dugans."

Dani and Peter spent their summers in the tree fort out back. They played that they were astronomers in a space ship. They played that they were explorers in the jungle. They played that they were a crocodile family living in the swamp. He wondered if they were ever simply going to pretend to be in a house. They never did. One day out of the blue, she said, "I love you, Peter. When we grow up, we are going to be married." She pushed him into the dad position of their make believe games. "You are the dad, Peter, you are the protector." Play became more fun for Peter after that. He fought the black knights. He chased the voracious dragons away. He returned with the treasure.

Peter chuckled now, thinking about her all these years later. He stretched in his car. Driving was slow with the snow. However, it gave him time to think and to remember. His Christmas deliveries were the one time of year he allowed himself to sink deep into his memories. They were full of might-have-been's and could-never-be's, but once a year, he let himself relive some of his happiest and saddest days.

When he was fourteen years old, the Dugans were planning a month-long vacation to Washington State. They asked his parents if he could come with them. The idea of actually going on a vacation was too much of a thrill to even think about for Peter. When his parents said yes—as long as he got a sub for his paper route—he was beside himself with joy. He didn't even mind that his clothes were old and stained. "Where are we going, Dani?"

"To Snoqualmie, Washington on the Skykomish River for a whole month. Look, I even have the travel guide that Mom bought."

This was a dream come true. Play with Dani was always exciting, but being with her in the forest left no limits for his imagination. And he had a goal. Even though Dani had told him she loved him, he had never returned the sentiment. But he loved her more than any person in his life. He was getting older, and he wanted to express his feelings toward her. Every time he planned to do it, he just couldn't get the words out. He was hoping on this trip he would find the courage to do it.

The first day there they went out to see the river. It was roaring with rapids from the spring runoff. They could see snow on the mountain peaks in the distance. Henry and Mary Dugan came out with them. "Okay, kids, this river is going to be a temptation. But you do not want to fall in. These rapids will carry you fast downstream to a huge waterfall. Even though you are good swimmers, the currents are too strong." Henry threw a stick in, and they all watched how fast it was swept by.

Dani backed away. "Let's hike up to the logger's swing they told us about." Mary gave Peter a small backpack with lunches and drinks inside. Dani rushed ahead as they followed the road deeper into the forest. Wild raspberries lined the road. "Hey, Dani, come back!" Peter called after her.

Dani returned looking peeved. Peter knew she didn't like to be distracted when she was on a mission. "What is it?" she asked. When she saw the berries, she took off her hat and used it as a bowl for collecting the berries. "Come on; let's find enough for a pie."

She ducked under the barbed-wire fencing and walked further into the woods, following the berries. They climbed up the mountain, going from one raspberry patch to the other. It was about 20 minutes later that they turned around with hats full of berries and realized they had no clue how to get back to the road. They tried one direction and stopped. Right in front of them was a baby bear. As soon as the bear saw them, he started hollering. That's when they heard a large animal rushing through the woods toward them.

Dani grabbed his hand. "Run!" They dropped their hats and ran as fast as they could, jumping over some fallen logs and tripping over others. Puffing and out of breath, Peter stopped first. "That bear is eating our berries."

Dani stopped next to Peter, hanging on his arm for support as she sucked in air. "She can have them. That was a close one. We could have been eaten ourselves."

Peter tentatively touched her arm. "I would have jumped in front of you, Dani. Then you could have gotten away."

Dani looked dumbfounded. "While the bear ate you? No, we could have both jumped on her back."

Peter started laughing. "It's not a horse, Dani."

Dani laughed harder and slapped her hip. "Ride 'em, cowboy!"

They both went into hysterics and fell back into a pile of pine needles under a large Ponderosa pine. Peter looked up into the tree, searching for bits of sky. He knew he would never forget this. "What are we going to say to your parents? They will not think it's one bit funny."

Peter was strictly obedient to the Dugans' rules. He did not want to do anything that would make them sorry they knew him.

"Well," Dani began, "we were minding our own business, picking raspberries for my mom to make raspberry pie, my dad's favorite, and this cute little baby bear came over and starting hollering for his mother. We knew that was bad news and started running for our lives. When we turned around, no one was chasing us."

Peter nodded. "That sounds good. But you left out the part where we got off the road and went into the woods."

Dani gave him one of those "Oh, brother!" looks.

Peter was still looking for ways to tell Dani he loved her, but figured being lost in the forest was not a good time.

Dani stood up and looked around. "Well, it's not going to matter what we say if we can't find our way back to tell the story."

"Let's eat our lunch here and then find the river." Peter took off his backpack, he was starving. They ate quickly and started walking downhill toward the sound of the river.

"Look, I can see the road from here." Dani pointed down the hill.

Looking down that hill made him a little dizzy; he wasn't good with heights. "I don't think I can go this way, Dani."

She shrugged and pointed the other direction. "We're not lost if we can see the road. Come on!" Dani led the way, and, as he always did in those days, Peter followed along. A large eagle swooped close over their heads and then dove toward the river. They lost sight of it behind some trees but then it rose back up, its powerful wings pumping hard to carry the weight of the large fish in its talons.

As they watched it glide to the other side of the canyon, Peter lost his footing and started to fall. His foot caught between two rocks, twisting his knee. It hurt like nothing he had ever felt before. Peter clenched his teeth and held in a scream.

"Peter!" Dani hurried down to him and helped him stand up. "Come on, that scared me." She had him lean on her while they half slid, half walked their way down to the bottom of the rockslide.

He tried to put more weight on his leg. It killed, but he tried not to show her. "Thanks, Dani, I can walk now." Deeper in the forest now, the trees blocked the sun, but here and there were tiny spots of sunlight that had managed to sneak through.

Peter remembered how grown up they felt as they opened the cabin door. They had been gone all day, avoided peril, and made it back in time for dinner. Dani's parents barely looked up as they welcomed them back. Dani looked at Peter conspiratorially. "They will start asking questions soon. Be ready."

No questions came. All night while playing Monopoly, Dani and Peter kept giving each other sneaky looks with raised eyebrows. Dani had a habit of talking with her hands, so every once in a while she would raise her hand palm up in question.

A semi whizzed past Peter on his way back to the airport, going at least seventy miles per hour, bringing him immediately back to the present. Peter shook his head. *They gave us way too much freedom in those days.* He and Dani could have gotten themselves killed a few times that month.

Peter thought back to the Washington trip. The very next day, they packed up their lunches and said they were going out exploring. They waited for some kind of response or advice or even a concerned look from her parents as they stepped out into the wild woods. But they just gave a slight wave and said, "Have a nice day."

As they walked back up the road, this time determined to make it to the logger's swing, Dani said, "Did you see my parents? I mean they could have at least warned us, like, 'Be careful, you could get eaten by a bear.' That would have been appropriate. Or maybe, 'Don't get lost in the woods. You could fall down a cliff!' "

"I guess they trust us." Peter knew not to say too much when Dani got on one of her rants.

"I don't want them to trust us; it's too much responsibility. They are supposed to know if it's safe here or not. They're parents. Now, I'm going to have to get the travel guide out and waste my vacation reading up on this place. We could be dead right now, or worse—we could be bear poop."

Peter followed, listening to her gripe. She was funny, and he needed to concentrate on something to avoid thinking about the pain in his knee. So he just nodded his head and agreed with everything she said as he silently dealt with the pain.

Peter slowed down as his jaguar slid a little to the side, going around a corner. A sports car was not the best idea for snow driving. The road curved through a tunnel of trees. The snow-covered branches looked like a winter wonderland in the reflection of his headlights.

It brought him back to the tunnel of trees they'd hiked through on their way to the logger's swing. It had been magical for a boy from the city. The smells were wonderful, and the fresh mountain air was invigorating. They found the logger's swing at the top of a hillside. A rope was connected to a swing that was hanging out over the canyon. They had to pull the swing back to the hill so they could get on and sail out over the tops of the trees.

He remembered Dani encouraging him to get on the swing. "You be first, Peter." Dani held the swing firm while he climbed on and then pushed him out over the canyon. The swing was attached high in the branches of a pine tree. He flew high over the tops of the other trees, and for the first time, he felt grateful for the pain in his knee—it kept his mind off of his terror from being up so high. "Get off after the first swing, or you will be stuck out there," Dani called.

His knee was killing him, but he dared not mention it in case the Dugans felt they should take him home. They played for hours and ate their lunch, looking out over the valley.

When Dani took her turn, she lay on her stomach as she sailed out over the tops of the trees. "I am Superwoman!" she screamed, the sound echoing over the canyon.

On their way home, they passed another cabin. Peter got the canteen out of the backpack. "I'm thirsty. Let's get some water at the river." They walked toward the water, where children were playing on rocks at the river's edge. Peter looked around for any adults as he bent down to fill his canteen.

Dani walked over to the kids. "Hi there, we're in the cabin down the way." The children waved and continued jumping from one rock to the other. Peter was just going to tell them to be careful when a little boy slipped, fell into the river, and was swept away. Peter dove in right behind him, reaching out to grab him. Dani ran as fast as she could downriver to an outcropping of rocks. Finally Peter got ahold of the boy, who was about four years old. He was choking and struggling to climb higher up Peter's body. "I've got you. Hold still."

He saw Dani wading out from the shore. She had her hand stretched out toward him. He kicked off one of the rocks and grabbed her hand. She pulled while he got a foothold, and they carried the boy to shore.

As soon as they put him down he ran to his cabin. Peter looked at Dani. They were both soaking wet. Her teeth were chattering. "You-you saved my life." He tried to show how sincere he was, how much he meant what he was about to say. "I love you."

He could still remember her wide, beautiful eyes staring up at him, partly amused and partly pleased. "I know you do, Peter. I love you too."

Now, all these years later, Peter knew he would always love Dani. His windshield wipers whipped as fast as they could, brushing snow aside so he could see. That summer he had had no idea how much his life was about to change.

Soon after that trip, his father was admitted to the hospital and died of liver failure. His mother just seemed to give up after that. It wasn't even a week later when she collapsed at work from a stroke. Peter stayed with the Dugans until his family from Connecticut sent someone to pick him up. The day he was to leave, the whole household was depressed. Henry told him he would have better advantages in life with his aunt but that they would sure miss him.

Dani and Peter rode their bikes to the park for the last time, to say their goodbyes in private. Dani put her arms around him, sobbing. She stepped away and then kissed him for the first time. It was the first kiss of a teenage love, but it awakened passions he knew nothing about. He desperately held her tight, never wanting to let her go. She broke away and ran to her bike. He cried out "bye" and watched her ride down the hill and out of his life.

The town butcher witnessed the scene and walked his dog over to Peter. "You will never be good enough for a girl like that." Peter looked down, not willing to look the man in the face.

The tall man reached down to pull back his small, snarling Shih Tzu. "You have bad blood." As he walked away, he looked back. "Sooner or later, you will end up just like your father."

Peter could feel the truth of those devastating words. What if Dani ended up like his mother? It crushed his heart. He determined he would never do anything to harm Dani, the only person he loved in the world.

When he got home from the park, there was a limo in front of his house. "Peter Jacobs, I am here on behalf of your aunt Meredith. My name is James. I already have your luggage, please get in." The Dugans were still at work. He had said goodbye the night before. He got in and felt the door close on what he thought would be the only happy time of his life.

James handed him a copy of the obituaries of his parents. They were simple. "Derrek Jacobs passed away due to complications associated with his illness." His mother's was even shorter. "Adelaide Walker Jacobs died of a brain aneurysm." As he rode hours on end to his new home, he wondered what his aunt would be like. His mother's sister was being forced to take him in. He hated to be a burden.

James told him that his aunt was a very busy woman and was in Europe at present. She had made arrangements for his education. "You are a very fortunate young man. Your schooling will be the best this country has to offer." As the limo drove up to a military academy, he was relieved. He wouldn't be a problem to her directly after all.

The campus was stately. The large red brick buildings reminded him of pictures he had seen of Independence Hall in Philadelphia. The sidewalks were lined with large, old maple trees. He liked the looks of the place. Uniformed boys were rushing along the sidewalks. As they got out of the limo, the tower clock began to chime. He followed James up the stairs to the head office. At the door, James shook his hand. He looked down at Peter and smiled kindly." You are going to do well here. I will probably see you again for holidays and summer breaks—if that is what your aunt decides." Peter clung to James's words of encouragement repeating them over and over in his mind. It gave him the courage he needed.

The school headmaster showed Peter into a room with uniforms that had been purchased for his use. When the headmaster looked at what was in his suitcase, he made a sour face. "Would you like me to throw these away for you?"

"Can I get a few keepsakes out first?"

"*May I*. And, yes, you may."

Dani had given him an arrowhead her father found in

Montana on a hunting trip. She said it would be a reminder of their love. He also took out a small wedding picture of his parents. It was the only remembrance of his mother that he had. In the bottom of his bag, tucked away almost as if he wanted to hide it from his memory was an eagle-embossed coin.

Looking at that coin the memory returned as it always did. Dani had always come bouncing over to his back door on Christmas morning to get Peter and bring him over to her house. On this particular morning, he woke up to hear his father screaming. He slowly crept down the hall toward the living room. His father was throwing furniture around, yelling over and over, "We killed them. We had to kill them!" His mother was trying to hold him back, but he threw her away, and she crashed into the wall and collapsed.

Peter ran over to her. "Mother, Mother!" She opened her eyes, and he helped her stand up. She walked over to his father, who had fallen back onto the sofa. "Derrek, it will be okay." She wiped his forehead and the drool that was hanging from his chin.

His father picked up a coin from the table and threw it toward Peter. "I never want to see this again." He then grabbed a bottle of whiskey and took a long drink.

Peter picked up the coin just as he heard Dani knock on the back door.

His mother nodded toward Peter. "You go ahead. I'm fine, and your dad feels better now. He's sick and suffering, Peter. It's okay." Peter looked at the coin and put it in his pocket. All he could see was the sorrow in his mother's eyes and the bleeding scratch on her forehead. She was the one that was sick and suffering, and it wasn't okay. It was the only time he struck her, that Peter knew of. She never had bruises or injuries. But every day must have been a trial to endure.

Peter looked over at the school master and put the coin in his pocket. His mother's suffering was over now. His father was dead, but Peter carried the poison of that moment in his blood.

"Let me show you to your room."

This was the beginning of his thirst for knowledge. He discovered he could gain recognition for doing well at school. The years passed quickly, and he graduated with honors. His aunt warmed to him as she saw him excel. He'd started to receive more holiday invitations to her home.

Letters came from Dani. He saved them but never responded. She was better off without him. He had looked up alcoholism, and the research was there. He did have bad blood.

It seemed his memories always ended with bad blood, the butcher and his snarling dog. Peter pulled himself back to the present, shaking the negative memories by humming along with the Christmas music for the last few miles to the airport where James, his pilot, waited.

CHAPTER 2

*C*hristmas morning arrived, and Dani got up early to make Sam's favorite pancakes. Her husband, Mitch, pushed his wheelchair to the living room to be there when Sam came out to open his gifts. "Is it going to be a good Christmas for Sam?" he asked.

"Sure, you know our parents always send a ton of gifts. He'll be thrilled." Dani finished setting the table.

After high school, marrying Mitch seemed the next logical step. Everyone expected that they would marry. At first their marriage was wonderful. Mitch had a good job managing a sporting goods store. And, before Sam was born, they traveled together to football games around the country.

She smiled as she remembered the fun their group of friends would have during the football season. Weekly BBQ's were scheduled to watch the games. It seemed, in their small town, you just kept the persona of your high school days. Mitch was still the football star, and she, the homecoming queen.

After a time, Dani wanted more than that. She hadn't finished college, and she wanted a family; soon she was pregnant. The joy of being pregnant was dampened when Mitch collapsed at a football game. He was admitted to the hospital and diagnosed with a severe case of early onset Parkinson's. She was in shock. Her world was crumbling before her. The next two weeks were a nightmare in and out of the hospital.

One afternoon, she was sitting on the front porch in the shade of a large maple tree when Mitch's boss drove up. He walked up the sidewalk, looking down. "Hello, Dani, I'm afraid I have some bad news. I received a message from headquarters. They're sending Mitch's replacement next week."

"He's fired? We just bought this house; what are we supposed to do now?" She'd known he would not be able to keep his job. But she'd hoped for something to come up. "So you don't have any office jobs that Mitch could do?

"I'm so sorry, we don't." His eyes held sympathy, but she could tell he was relieved to get back in his car and drive away.

This was just the first of many disappointments. "Mitch, my friends never call now. I think Sherrie was avoiding me at the grocery store last week. We are not invited to the football parties anymore either," she said one evening when she was tired of pretending everything was normal. "You can see clearly who your real friends are when something like this happens."

"Who wants a sick, dying guy at their party? Talk about a letdown."

Dani could see the truth of what he said, but admitting it just made it worse. It locked her into the situation with no way to get out. She was too positive a person to admit defeat. "You are not dying. They have more medicines to try. People can live many years with this disease. There are even celebrities with this disease."

Mitch tossed his sports magazine on the floor. "I don't like being around the group anymore, Dani. Not when they don't really want me there."

"Well, I love you, and I want to be with you, so we'll just spend time with people who appreciate us and do everything we can to keep you here."

She was trying so hard to keep him happy she didn't recognize her own fall into depression until her OB mentioned it. "Dani, I know you have a hard family situation. You also have a baby that needs the best nutrition your body can give. You don't want to take medicine for depression during your pregnancy."

"Why would I do that?" Dani was surprised by his comment.

"Dani, you are obviously depressed. I see all the signs. As hard as this is, you can't let this get you down. I want you to start walking at least three miles a day. If the weather is bad, go to the gym or even the mall and walk. You are becoming a shadow of the person you once were."

Dani broke down and cried for the first time since Mitch's diagnosis. Her OB had been a good friend in high school. They'd been debate partners. He put his arm on her shoulder. "It's good to cry. I bet you never do anything for yourself these days."

Dani laughed through her tears. "How did you know?"

She felt much better after her appointment. She had to get a grip. She read in one of her pregnancy books that a stressed mother could make her baby more prone to stress. If she was going to be a good mother, she needed to start now.

She went home that day and took a serious look at their finances. She figured she had enough in the bank to make house payments for two more months—until the end of the year. That gave her time to try and figure something out. Her parents had encouraged her to come and live with them, but she wasn't ready to give up her independence, not yet.

One day in December, just as she returned home from her daily walk, she found the bank manager sitting in his car out in front of her house. He got out when he saw her and handed her a letter. "Dani, an anonymous benefactor has paid off your mortgage. We received this letter from our headquarters in New York. You will find the deed with the other paperwork."

Dani sank to sit on the porch steps. "Who would do this? And how can I possibly thank them."

"I don't know, but seeing this sure gives me the Christmas spirit." He smiled at her. "Merry Christmas, Dani." He got into his car and drove away.

"Merry Christmas!" she called after him. She sat down just inside the door and opened the letter. She could not believe what she was reading. The letter stated that just as he said, a benefactor had paid off the mortgage on their home. Dani fell back onto the sofa, crying with relief. Once the tears stopped, she whooped with joy.

Mitch was in the hospital again for testing. The meds he had been taking were not working any longer. She showered and rushed to the hospital to tell him the good news. He read the letter over a couple times and smiled. "You will be okay, now. I have been so worried."

"Mitch, *we* will make it now. We can do this! This is the perfect Christmas!"

After they changed his medicines, Mitch started to feel better. But he became less communicative and kept to his room longer each day.

Sam was born that spring. At the hospital, Dani held her new baby close as she shed a tear. Could she protect him from his life's sorrows? Mitch was failing fast, and she was afraid this little boy wouldn't get to know his father. All at once, she could see Peter's destitute expression as he'd received news of each of his parent's deaths. She shed a tear for him too, remembering their tender goodbye years ago.

Mitch did have that much wished for remission from his illness and the years passed in happiness. He participated more in the family and kept up an internet job. The secret gifts arrived every year, sometimes by delivery and sometimes they found them on the front porch. One year she received a scholarship to a university that had online degrees. She was thrilled and enrolled immediately. But most of the gifts were for Sam. She had come to feel like she had a guardian angel somewhere out there. It gave her a sense of peace and comfort through all the uncertainty.

The Woodlock home was always the most brightly decorated house on their street. Yearly, her parents sent her a box of decorations from the ranch. She always laughed, thinking she could decorate the entire grade school with her Christmas loot.

Her parents owned the Rio Lago Ranch. She loved it there. It was a high end ranch resort. There was a little cottage behind the ranch house, in a grove of trees, that was hers any time she came. It was away from the guests and had a huge swing and little playground for Sam. She had only been home once since he was born. With Mitch's illness, she hated to leave him home alone, and he didn't want to travel.

She let her mind roam through her memories while she finished making the pancakes and decided she had a good life. She felt satisfied and grateful. Finally, Sam came downstairs with bright eyes as he surveyed the presents under the tree.

"Boy, Sam, I wondered if I was going to have to wake you up on Christmas morning. Merry Christmas!" Dani gave him a big hug, and he ran over to his Dad for another.

Her parents always sent fun gifts for Christmas. She wished she could have been home with them this year. Mitch had been in remission for the last few years but his prognosis now was getting worse. Her parents couldn't come up—Christmas was a busy time at her parents' dude ranch. She sighed knowing she wouldn't have their help as she tried to make Christmas fun for Sam.

As Sam went over to look at his presents, he squealed with delight. He carefully lined up each gift on the table.

It was a tradition in their family that Mitch told the Christmas story from the Bible at breakfast on Christmas morning. This year Dani did it. Whole wheat, fluffy pancakes filled Sam up, and he asked to go outside to see the snow. It was a special Christmas if Kentucky received snow. Dani bundled him up and opened the door to the porch. She turned away but stopped when she heard Sam yell. She looked back. He was beaming, standing next to a beautiful, red bike.

Dani stepped out. "Where did that come from?" Dani looked around the street. Everything was magically white with snow. There was no sign of Santa's helper.

"It was Santa, Mom. He told me at the mall that I could have any wish I wanted."

"I'm starting to think you are right, Sam."

CHAPTER 3

*P*eter drove to the airport hangar where the pilot of his Learjet waited. He rented this particular hangar full time so he could leave his Jaguar in its place to wait for next year's Christmas delivery to Dani. At the estate he had a garage full of cars; some he purchased but a few were left by his uncle George that his aunt hadn't wanted to sell.

"Thanks, James, I appreciate these Christmas trips you take with me."

James smiled and taxi'd the jet out of the hangar. "These trips make Christmas real to me. Having these secret deliveries is not only fun it's a part of Christmas that I look forward to."

"I really appreciate the help and good advice you've given me over the years. And besides who can say their limo driver is also their pilot?" Peter laughed.

James laughed. "Only the people who pay like you do."

Peter reached into his brief case and pulled out a carved

wooden box. "That reminds me, here's your Christmas bonus." James opened the lid and found it was full of gold coins.

"Thanks, Peter, I may have to start burying this loot." James laughed. "Before you take your seat, have you thought about what I said last year about contacting Dani? You're not the pariah you once believed you were." James leaned back to look him directly in the eye.

"She is happily married, and I won't do anything to upset that." He frowned, thinking of her and her husband's illness.

"Well, it is good that you can help her now and then. Even though you are not a part of her life, you've still taken steps to support her life whenever you can. It shows where your heart is."

"That's all I can do now." Peter took the arrowhead and his dad's coin out of his pocket. Deep down he still felt that nagging butchers voice. This was all he should ever do.

Peter shut the cabin door and took his seat.

He sat back, satisfied with this year's Christmas trip. It was getting harder to figure out things that Sam might want to have. His mall Santa idea had helped, but Sam wasn't going to believe in Santa for too much longer.

At thirty, Peter had dated a few women, but he still compared everyone he met to Dani. *Sleek Magazine* had voted him the most eligible bachelor of the season. He had dark curly hair, cut a little long. He was 6'7", and he stayed in pretty good shape. He had been a runner at school and spent every morning working out. The fact that he never touched alcohol allowed him to skip the middle age belly most of his work associates were gaining. He was also the richest bachelor in New York at present. He tended to avoid social events just for that reason.

He was an impressive business leader in New York and had the respect of the community. As CEO of his Aunt's hedge fund Peter had doubled revenue since he had taken charge. His aunt was more than happy to have him manage the business. Time and again, people hinted or out right nudged him to date, to settle down. But he resisted.

When they landed, he saw his aunt's limo waiting on the tarmac. James laughed as he opened the door. "Looks like Aunt Meredith wants a meeting."

Peter packed up his briefcase and headed down the stairs. "She's keeps life interesting, James. I enjoy talking with her." He gripped his old friend's hand and thanked him again. "Merry Christmas James."

He stepped off the plane and the new driver, Clark, opened the door. "Welcome back, sir."

"Thanks, Clark." Peter climbed in. "Hello, Aunt Meredith." He leaned over to kiss her cheek.

"Hello, Peter, I do miss you on Christmas day. I have ordered it for tomorrow instead." She laughed and patted his arm affectionately.

"That is a marvelous idea." He loved this hard, sophisticated woman. She had softened toward him over the years. After his graduation from Harvard, she told him, "I am proud to be your aunt." This compliment was akin to being anointed at Westminster Abby. After his graduation, she had regular business meetings with him, and he was expected for every Sunday dinner. Three years later she had asked him to move into the east wing of the estate.

"Aunt, how are you feeling today." The lines on her face had softened, but she was getting more of them and looked tired most days.

His aunt put her hand on his cheek. "Don't worry about me, Peter, I'm fine." Even at this age, she was a very beautiful woman. She carried herself like a queen and had kept herself looking young and trim.

As they drove into the estate, Peter marveled that all this was his. "Aunt, do you intend to keep these hunting acres wild and natural?"

His aunt became flustered. "I am not going to have a cavalcade of horses and hounds hunting the place like the last occupant." The estate possessed 20 acres of hunting grounds. But his aunt had turned it into an animal refuge during the hunting season to the chagrin of her neighbors.

The rest of the estate was manicured gardens with appropriately placed ponds and waterfalls. There was an inside and an outside pool, with tennis courts behind the pool. And the estate sat north of New London on the Atlantic shore. Peter helped his aunt out of the limo once they arrived home. "Christmas begins at 11 am sharp Peter." She chuckled but meant it.

Aunt Meredith's Christmas day did begin at 11 a.m. sharp. She had asked for a painting of him for Christmas, and he had sat patiently while her choice of artist captured his portrait. Each year she told him exactly what she wanted from him as a gift, which he greatly appreciated.

They sat down to brunch. "Merry Christmas, Aunt. You look lovely this morning." He had the painting set out and asked Edgar to remove the sheeting.

"Oh, Peter, it's wonderful! He captured your brilliance. You have your mother's eyes."

A sadness came over her face then. She dabbed her eyes with her napkin. "Edgar, leave it here for now, but I would like that hung in my sitting room."

"Of course, ma'am."

"Come follow me, Peter. I have your present this way."

Aunt Meredith walked him to the west wing and opened the door to the library.

"This is fabulous! How did you have this done without me knowing?"

"I have a sneaky contractor." She grinned. "And let me tell you, he moaned about the restrictions I put on his workers. But he didn't mind the Christmas bonus I gave him."

Peter looked around the room. A large desk was situated back by new French doors that opened onto a patio and garden. The far wall was floor-to-ceiling glass, three remaining walls held bookshelves already full of books he was sure his aunt expected him to read. "Aunt, I love this. You couldn't have surprised me more."

He and his aunt spent the rest of the evening playing Parcheesi, one of her favorite games.

Two days after their Christmas dinner his aunt met him at breakfast with a command. "You will now take a trip to visit all the estates. Bradley and Beck will go with you so you can meet the staff and get to know your holdings." He knew better than to argue with her when her mind was made up.

"I will go in to work today to settle some things and clear my schedule. I could probably leave the end of the week. Would you want to accompany me?" Peter remembered how often she had traveled to the continent while he was growing up.

"No dear boy, my traveling days are over. I am most content to stay here now. However, I will be anxious to hear what you think of the European estates when you get back."

The end of the week he took the family jet to each of the European estates. He was amazed at the luxury that sat empty most of the time. The staffs had been most reliable and very happy to meet him. Of all the estates the one in England impressed him the most even though it was the most modest of the three.

The England estate was located on the Thames River. The home originally belonged to the head of Gayhurst School and was named Little Gayhurst. It was located between the towns of Bourne End and Cookham. The property had its own boat launch and seemed to be in good shape. As he walked out back to see the one-hundred-year-old red maple tree, he asked, "Is that golf course across the river popular among the residents?" His lawyers assured him it was and offered to take him golfing the next day.

The grounds were surrounded with a large twelve-foot-high wall. To discourage anyone from trying to climb over, sharp broken glass had been embedded year ago into the concrete on top. The caretaker, who was living in the apartment over the garage, was not looking after the property as well as Peter would have liked. He was getting on in age and could use help. "Mr. Wright," he said to the caretaker, "I am planning to hire a couple gardeners for you to manage. I would expect them to do all the garden work and keep the shoreline clean and presentable. It will be good for you to have a small staff to take care of issues you may not want to do yourself."

Mr. Wright sighed in relief. He was a stout, shorter man with silver-grey hair and a jolly, weathered face. His wife stood next to him. They were the picture of a devoted pair. Peter liked them immediately and was happy to have such high-caliber people tending to his estate.

"Thank you, sir, I was worried I might be losing my position."

"No, sir. Mr. Beck will sit down with you today and discuss your salary increase. And he has a retirement plan for you as well that he will go over. You may have the use of the apartment for as long as you need it."

The Wrights both smiled through teary eyes. "Thank you so much. We will do our best."

Peter shook Mr. Wright's hand. "I can see that you already are."

Before they left the estate, Peter took one more walk out to the river's edge. The Thames was wide at this point, and he could see a father and son jogging along a path on the other side. He wondered if he would ever be so fortunate as to have a son. Peter spent the flight home working.

He felt good about the trip he had taken with the lawyers. He was very attached to his aunt and happy their relationship had grown close over the years. She was the closest person he had to his mother, and watching his aunt gave him a glimpse of what his mother could have been had she not ended up with his father.

Peter considered all he has seen on each estate. "Mr. Beck how often are these estates visited now?"

"Well, Mr. Jacobs, this is the first visit in two years." Peter wondered how his aunt would feel about selling at least one of them.

Peter was quiet the rest of the trip. He kept thinking about James' suggestion that he try to visit Dani. Of course he would never do that while she was married. He knew his fear of destroying her life was not all together rational. He hadn't taken a drink his entire life. The chances of him ever doing so were slim yet he couldn't rid himself of the pit in his stomach every time he even thought about a life with her. And who was to say whether she would even be interested in him. Maybe he needed a therapist.

CHAPTER 4

Someone delivered a goose to Dani's home on Christmas Eve. She smiled. This was the second Christmas goose that had mysteriously been delivered to her doorstep. Her mother had sent a Martha Stewart recipe for goose with rice stuffing. She loved the smell of it cooking. Mitch had fallen asleep in his chair, and Dani sat down in the window seat to watch Sam ride his bike outside. She chuckled, thinking of how anxious he'd been for the snow to melt. He had tried to take her hair dryer outside to speed up the process. "Sam, I promise the snow will be melted by noon. This is Kentucky after all."

Her home was lovely. She had very nice western-style furniture. Much of it came from her parents' ranch resort. Each year they remodeled some of the hotel rooms and sent her a truckload of furnishings. Furnishings from a five-star dude ranch made her home the best furnished in the neighborhood. She'd complained the first year at how much furniture they sent. "Mom, what am I supposed to do with all of this?"

"Why, Dani, have a garage sale of course."

After that first year, she just gave up and gladly accepted the truck's contents. Her living room had big leather sofas. There was a large coffee table sitting on gnarled cedar legs with a large glass shadow box top filled with western paraphernalia; arrowheads, small Native American artwork, old gold coins and spurs. Sam could sit for hours, imagining stories for each piece.

She had a bearskin rug in the office that startled her when she entered the room more often than not. The memory of her and Peter being chased by a bear popped up now and then when she went in there. Thinking of those long claws and sharp teeth made her cringe at what could have happened. They were so carefree and clueless in those days. She determined not to be so cavalier with Sam's safety.

Sam came running into the house. "Mom, I'm starved, I need a cookie."

"This isn't Grandma's house, Sam. You can have a deviled egg while we wait for the goose to finish cooking."

"Yuck! That's disgusting."

Dani laughed and ruffled his hair. "I think we'll eat in about 15 minutes. Can you wait that long?"

Dani sat in the recliner at the side of her work desk. She loved the glass-encased bookshelves that came with the desk. Her dad had included many of the latest New York Times bestsellers and classics they liked to stock for guests.

A cowboy and horse set decorated Sam's room. The chair in his room was a saddle on a carved wooden horse. It was huge, and was another gift they had found on the front porch one Christmas morning. Sam's room had a large llama rug with pictures of wolves, cows, and coyotes on the wall. The matching pottery, artwork, lamps, draperies and area rugs for each room were all from her parents.

When the truck came each year, she would take what she wanted and have a huge garage sale for everything else. Last week, she had opened her front door to find three women standing on her porch. "Hello, Dani, we have a suggestion we would like you to consider." The whole town looked forward to the truck's arrival, and they asked if they could set up a bazaar along the street next year. These shipments were officially becoming a town event.

Mitch interrupted her thoughts and called to her from the other room. "Dani, we need to talk. You have been avoiding this long enough." Dani dreaded the conversation she knew he wanted to have.

She walked over to him, her heart in pain, and sat on the arm of the chair next to him. "I know, Mitch, I just keep thinking something will happen and all this bad news will change for the better."

"I'm stage five, Dani, you know what that means."

"I've been studying up, and I think I can take care of you." She smiled encouragingly.

"Dani, how are you going to get me out of bed and into the chair? There was a reason I played football."

"A crane!" she answered. Mitch rolled his eyes in exasperation.

"No, seriously, I have looked into it. They have cranes for situations like this." She had to smile a little; it was a bit outrageous sounding.

Mitch started laughing. "Well, who operates this crane? I'm

envisioning you lifting me up, swinging me over and dropping me on the floor."

They both laughed. He had a point.

"And then who will pick me up?" he asked.

"Well, you would still have the sling around you; we would just try again." She raised her eyebrows hopefully.

Mitch shook his head.

"So, we talked. Are you happy now, honey?" Dani stood up.

"Not too much." Mitch had a wry smile. "But at least you're back to being the determined and stubborn woman I married."

Dani leaned down behind him and put her arms around his neck. "We will think of something."

Dani called Sam in for Christmas dinner. He brought his bike into the house and to his bedroom after he dried it with one of her nice towels from the ranch.

The goose was wonderful. There wasn't much of it, but it was perfect for her small family. Sam was getting better at trying new foods. He actually loved the sweet potatoes—better described as brown sugar with a dollop of sweet potato smothered in marshmallows.

Dani cleaned up after dinner storing away left overs. Sam complained, "Will I have to eat this again?"

"Well, the day after Christmas is special for moms. I make a big dinner on Christmas so there are lots of yummy leftovers. Then I don't have to cook again the next day, and we'll have more time to play with all of your Christmas presents."

Sam loved to just sit, snuggled up with his Mom, and listen to her tell stories. Sometimes she told him stories of her exploits with Peter. He said they were his favorite.

Dani waited a couple weeks after Christmas to call her parents. She missed them so much, she almost hated to call. Every year it was the same thing. She always felt such a loss when she hung up.

But now most of the winter rush was over at the resort and she could have a leisurely conversation with them. They were always swamped with guests over the holidays. "Hi, Mom, merry Christmas!"

"Dani, dear, merry Christmas. We are finally getting a break here. Did Sam like the toys we sent?"

"Yes, he loved the toys, Mom. But you were outdone again by Santa. There was a beautiful, red BMX bicycle on the front porch this morning."

"Have you ever figured out who's doing this? It's not us, although I wish it was."

"I have no idea. I honestly have stopped thinking about it. Sam said it was Santa. I am going to have to go with that."

Her mother paused dramatically. "You will never guess who we ran into on our trip to New York. It was Peter! We were so happy to see him."

"Peter? Really? How is he doing?" Dani's heart jumped. She was surprised by the empty feeling in the pit of her stomach. He had dropped out of her life when he left to live with his aunt. She remembered sitting in her tree fort, writing letter after letter. It hurt each time the mail came and there were no letters from Peter. Eventually she pushed memories of him to the back of her mind, deciding it was childish to hold on to a friendship that was not returned.

"We invited him to join us, so he sat down and spent about an hour with us. He looks great. He has turned into a very handsome man, a lot like his father. There is an air of confidence about him. He seemed happy and talked fondly of his aunt Meredith."

"Does he have a family now? I assume he's married."

"We asked him that. He said he wasn't, but he had someone special in mind."

"I am very happy for him." Dani's ire was up a little at hearing this. Her whole life she had a hard time when things didn't turn out like she had planned. Peter had been supposed to write when he went away. For years they had sat in that tree fort and made plans for their future. She had had it all worked out. And then he just dropped out of her life. She had scolded him in her letters for his unfaithful behavior. She laughed. It was all pretty childish, but she couldn't help feeling thwarted anyway.

"We all took a selfie together. I will text it to you."

"Thanks, Mom. Is Dad there?"

"He's out at the barn. I'll have him call you later tonight."

Dani's phone dinged, and she looked at the picture of her parents and Peter.

Whoa! Her mom wasn't kidding. He was gorgeous. She couldn't believe he wasn't married. How could any woman let him pass by? Dani looked closer and those same kind eyes stared back at her.

Mitch rolled in next to her. "How are your parents doing?"

"They're great. Look at this picture of them in New York." She handed him the phone.

"They are certainly aging gracefully. Something about ranch work keeps you young, I guess. Who's the guy?"

"That's Peter."

"Hmm. You never once mentioned his looks."

"No, he was different then. His whole countenance has changed. He seems more in control somehow. I don't know. But whatever changed, it was for the good. The last time I saw him, he was a scared, beaten-down kid."

"Well he has had quite the revival."

Dani smiled at her husband's reaction. She took her phone back and pinched his cheek playfully. Mitch had always been pretty territorial when it came to her.

Sam had one more day left of his school holiday and it was Friday movie night. Mitch promised him they could watch the movie *Cars* together. Dani had seen it at least 20 times while Sam was growing up. So she went to the office and shut the door.

She sat back in the recliner and looked at the picture of Peter again. A happy peace settled on her heart. He was doing fine. All these years, she had worried about him. Before he left she had made it her job to see that he was okay. She smirked. She had even beaten up a couple boys who had been bullying him. She didn't tell Sam those stories. Who wants a mom who beats up boys?

It felt really good to sit and look into Peter's confident, happy face. He didn't need her help now.

CHAPTER 5

*D*ani liked to leave the Christmas decorations up at least until after New Year's Day. Christmas was such a wonderful happy time, and with Mitch's continued decline, they needed whatever happiness they could squeeze out of the holidays this year. The doctor told them it would be his last. But Dani just couldn't bring herself to give up. Surely there would be a new medicine they could try. She constantly researched new therapies. She made a point of preparing the freshest healthy food she could find. Her parents had sent a high powered blender so she could blend up his food now that it was so hard for him to eat. It was her nature to fight back, but no matter what she did, he still continued to decline.

One morning in March, she watched Sam get on the bus and then quickly put a load of laundry in. The month before, a hospital bed was delivered, and Mitch had started sleeping in the spare bedroom. She spent most of her nights in there, as well, on the recliner. She went to the kitchen to make a protein smoothie for Mitch and started the dishwasher. As she was coming down the hall, she took a sudden intake of breath. And she knew. She looked at his bedroom door, and her heart filled with fear. *Mitch, not today.* She put the drink on the hall table and continued to his door.

As she came in the room, she knew he was going to leave her. "Mitch, stay!" She sat gently on his bed and held his hand. "Don't go!"

He shook his head and whispered. "I love you, Dani. Tell Sam." His breath was ragged, but his face filled with peace.

"I love you too. I will, I will."

He turned his head and looked at the doorway and smiled. "Hey, Grandpa."

And then he was gone. Her heart clenched. The fell across his chest and ached for the life he could have had, for all the missed years, for afternoons of throwing the football with Sam, everything he would have loved and was gone. She ached for his humor and even his strength in his life, before that too had dwindled over the years. And she cried for her own burdens. For the moment she would have to tell Sam. She held his hand until it felt cold and then she called the hospital.

Everyone in the town attended the funeral. Her parents and all of Mitch's extended family flew in from all over the country. The minister knew Mitch growing up and told a few football stories from his glory days. He shared scriptures of the promised resurrection. Dani kept thinking about Mitch's last words. He'd definitely thought he saw his grandfather. She kept thinking about it. Had his grandfather come to get him? That was a very reassuring thought.

At the end of the service, people filed up to the front and greeted the family. The last person came forward just as she was telling Sam he could go sit down. She looked up and gasped. "Peter. Peter!" She took his hand.

"Dani, I was so sorry to hear about Mitch. The funeral was a great tribute to a great man."

"Thank you." Seeing Peter in person was far more powerful than seeing his picture. He was a force. Dani felt weak. He was so much taller than she was. But then, out of nowhere, irritation surged.

"You never answered my letters."

"I didn't think I would get chewed out for that the first time I saw you. I thought I would be safe at the funeral at least." Peter laughed.

"This is funny?" she asked. *He has such a great smile, and he looks so happy. I am being such an idiot.*

"I'm sorry," Dani apologized. "That was a long time ago." Dani was genuinely happy for Peter. She hoped he would be very happy with the girl he'd mentioned to her parents. It was comforting to see him.

"A lot has happened, Dani. Sometime I would like to get together and share it with you."

"I'm going to spend a few months at my parent's ranch in Texas. They'd love to spend time with you again, I'm sure. Maybe then?"

"Maybe. I look forward to seeing you again." He smiled and turned to leave.

She stood there deep in thought, watching him as he walked out the front door of the church.

The usher escorted her to the limo where her parents and Sam were waiting.

The small town cemetery looked like a pasture with white board fencing all around. All the headstones were flat against the ground, so from a distance, it truly did look like a lovely green pasture. There were large oak trees providing shade at each corner. She really hated the idea of having Mitch put in the ground, even in such a lovely spot. His family had asked that he be buried in their family section of the cemetery. Dani was happy with that. She reached down and put her arm around Sam. They walked over to the burial spot and sat in the chairs by the casket.

Sam took the handkerchief Dani handed to him and blew his nose. "I am glad that he isn't sick anymore, Mom."

"Me too." Dani put her arm around him. "How would you like it if we went to stay with Grandma and Grandpa for a while?"

"Can I bring my bike?"

Dani smiled, he was going to be okay. "Yes, honey, you can bring your bike and any toys you want."

Mitch had been a good husband and father. They loved each other and had made the best of their situation. She had no regrets. She had done everything she could to be a good and supportive wife. Mitch had thanked her for that many times. Now here she was, beginning a new chapter of her life. It would be good to go home to Texas to heal, to remember him, and take stock of her options.

Dani rented a small U-Haul trailer. Sam's toys took up most of the room, but she had a few things she needed to bring as well.

She had planned to create some photobooks of their family pictures but never had the time. Now that she was going to be at the ranch she hoped she would have time. *I am going to keep your memory alive, Mitch.* The books were the first step. It would be healing to go through those memories.

As she walked through her house one more time, she had a feeling she would never live there again. What her future held was in the unknown realm, but whatever it was, she was determined to grasp it and hold on.

It took two days to drive down to the ranch in Texas. She laughed as she drove along the highway in front of her parents' resort. It looked shabbier than ever. They were really taking this private resort thing seriously. No one would think this was a place celebrities would actually stay.

Sam looked wide-eyed. "Is this where Grandpa lives?" He was probably too young to remember.

"Sam, Grandpa likes to play dress-up with the ranch. He pretends it's a really old, broken-down place."

As they got out of the car, Dani's mom came running with her arms open wide. Sam jumped out of the car and into her loving arms. "Grandma! I love it here already. You have real horses!"

Dani's dad, Henry, walked up. "Wait till you taste her cookies!"

Dani collapsed into her dad's arms. "Oh, Dad, I have missed it here so much. You and Mom have made a little paradise. It will be good to stay a while and regain my balance."

"You can stay as long as you want. That little house out back is yours. We had it all remodeled, and everything is new. If you don't like the furnishings, just come over here and choose what you want."

Carson walked over and gave Dani a hug. "I'm sorry to hear about Mitch. He was a good man."

"Thank you, Carson. I have missed those riding lessons." She turned to her son. "Sam, this is Carson. He is the cowboy I was telling you about."

Sam peered up at Carson. "Are you a real cowboy?"

"I sure am, and I need a partner around here. Are you interested in the job?"

Sam looked up at Dani with eyes begging her to say yes. "Sure, Sam," she said, "But ranching is hard work, and being a cowboy is the biggest job there is."

"Waahooey!" He ran to the car to get his cowboy hat.

Henry turned to Carson. "Can you get some hands to unload this trailer at Dani's house out back?"

Dani's mom, Mary, gave her a hug and called them all into dinner. "Carson, you come too."

After dinner, Dani said goodnight. She walked down the path to her little house nestled back in the trees. There was a big *welcome home* sign on the new front porch. "Oh look, Sam, we have a front porch." He ran up and climbed into the porch swing. The front door opened, and Juanita, the cook, and her daughter came out with empty grocery bags. "We stocked your cupboards and refrigerator with lots of good food. I hope you don't mind that we also got you unpacked."

"Oh, Juanita, you are wonderful! Thank you!" *Bless these women.* The house was perfect. The cute little kitchen had the newest appliances available. She noticed they had put in a new picture window in the living room, facing the woods. They had also opened up the kitchen wall with sliding doors to a newly built deck. "Wow, Dad went to town on this one." She jerked in alarm when she almost stepped on the bear's head in the office. "Oh no, another bear rug." She wondered if this bear was any relation to the bear that chased her and Peter that day.

Sam was thrilled, running room to room. Finally he settled down and went to his bedroom to read. Dani took a few minutes to set up her computer. She sat down and sighed, and for the first time in days, relaxed. She immediately fell asleep in the office recliner.

CHAPTER 6

onths went by, and as always Dani was never far from Peter's thoughts. He sought for ways to create more meaning in his life. When James came to Peter with an idea for a boys club, Peter loved it. There were many boys out there who didn't have a Dugan family to help them. The building they purchased had everything a typical YMCA would have—a swimming pool, tennis and racquet ball courts, and a game room. They hired a manager with childcare credentials and met with him weekly to plan the activities they would offer. Peter came to the meetings at James's request, but he had full confidence in James to oversee the project. His charitable character and business sense were just what the club needed. Since they began the project, James seemed happier and had added purpose to his step.

Seeing James happy made him happy. The man had been like a father to him. And he struggled. James' triumphs over his own addictions were a constant beacon of hope to Peter.

And with his own work under control, life was going pretty well.

Then one morning at breakfast, his aunt looked over at him with a small, tentative smile. "Peter, I would like you to meet with an accomplished woman who has a good business idea for the city."

Oh no, another matchmaking attempt.

"Sure, Aunt Meredith. I was looking for something to work on for the city." He wasn't ready to date anyone, but figured, why not. His heart had already been given to Dani, and he didn't see that changing. But he was open to the possibility of someone else, someday. He didn't plan to stay single forever. So he dressed with particular care and drove into the city.

That evening Peter walked into Le Bernardin, the Midtown restaurant his aunt raved about, famous for its French seafood dishes. The atmosphere was luxurious. He loved seafood, so he would at least enjoy the meal portion of this meeting.

Peter was shown to his table and had only waited a few minutes when he looked up and saw a beautiful woman walking toward him. She was tall and slender with long red hair that was lightly highlighted. She looked directly at him and smiled. He stood up while she was seated. She reached out her hand, business-like. "Hello, I am Jessica Wixom."

This was the first time he'd been at a business meeting that was also a prospective date. He took her hand. "Thank you for coming, Peter Jacobs." This woman was a force all her own. She seemed totally confident of her place in this world.

He ordered a dish with a variety of fish presentations. It all looked good. She ordered a salad. Women could be so impractical. She was here at a great fish house and she ordered a salad that she could get anywhere. Surely fish wasn't outside the bounds of whatever diet she was on. He sighed.

When they had eaten, he asked her about her business proposal. She went into an overly rehearsed pitch. "We need backers for a bike rental system throughout Manhattan, similar to the luggage racks at the airport."

He tried to bring her out of her pitch and back into a conversation. "Have you checked into city approval?"

"Not yet, I want to go to them with a proposal backed up with funding." She jumped back into her monotone pitch. Peter looked at his phone, no messages. She continued her speech, much of which Peter wasn't listening to. He looked at this woman and imagined Dani sitting there. She would be animated if she were giving this presentation, and she wouldn't put up with his indifference for a second. And if he'd looked at his phone, she probably would have taken it away. He laughed at that.

Jessica stopped, confused. "We were hoping you would be one of them."

"I am sorry, Jessica, I do like this idea. Why don't I have my lawyers take a look at it? They have contacts on the city council, and we will see where it goes from there."

He stood and helped her with her chair.

"Thank you, Mr. Jacobs. I really appreciate it."

"I will have my secretary contact you once we talk with the city council."

After the dinner, she went her way and he asked his driver to take him downtown. Driving was always a good time to reminisce. Being with another woman this evening only brought on thoughts of Dani. She always had a big project she wanted to do. They used to spend hours planning, and they'd always executed their plans. Not to do so would have been a disaster in her eyes.

His mind drifted back to their time in Washington. At the cabin, Dani decided to read the travel guide. "In order to save our lives —since my parents are unconcerned about our safety—I have decided to read up on this place." While reading, she discovered there were lots of caves in the area. That was all she needed. This time, as they headed out for the day, they had flashlights, compasses, matches, and a pair of binoculars along with their lunches. They were going caving. Every day for three days, they scoured the mountains. On the fourth day, she finally spotted what looked like a cave.

Dani handed Peter the binoculars. "Here, Peter, look up there." She adjusted the direction he was looking. "No, over there. See that dark spot?" He looked and finally found it. Her excitement was persuasive, and they both headed up the mountain with a jump in their step, at least for the first mile. The woods were getting darker as they hiked. Birds were screeching their objection all along the way, but all of a sudden it became quiet.

Peter stopped. "Something is wrong. It's too quiet." They looked around and decided to hide just in case. They climbed under the bottom branches of a smaller pine tree until they were sitting next to the trunk. It was kind of cozy under there, and they were completely covered. Then they heard something coming through the woods. As it got closer, they could hear voices. Dani's sharp intake of breath caused his gut to twist."Look, Peter, it's a cougar. They killed a cougar." The men had the legs of the mountain lion tied around a stick they were carrying between them on their shoulders. The cougar was hanging from her feet. It was plain she had been nursing kittens. A profound sadness descended upon him. "I feel horrible."

He looked at Dani; she had tears running down her cheeks. She leaned over and curled up against him. He carefully put his arm around her while she cried. After a time, she sniffed and wiped her eyes. "We're going to do something about this. Come on!"

They climbed out and started up the mountain, following the heavy footprints of the hunters. "If we follow their trail, maybe we'll find her kittens. The mommy cougar would be happy that we saved her babies."

"What if there is a daddy cougar?" After the bear episode, he was not too keen on making friends with wildlife.

"I don't think the daddy stays home. The mom chases him away, I think."

They had only gone about ten feet when they saw two tiny cougar kittens following the path their mother had taken down the mountain. Her blood was still fresh in the grass and dirt. Peter immediately sat down in the middle of the path. He put out his hands and called to the kittens. "Come on, kitty, we will help you. Come on, kitty."

The kittens both stopped then took a tentative step toward Peter. Dani dropped down as well and started calling softly. It took about an hour, but finally they were comfortable enough that Dani and Peter picked them up and wrapped them in their jackets.

They stood up and looked at each other, eyes sparkling. "We did it!" Even in Peter's wildest imaginations, he had never thought anything like this would ever happen to him.

"Yes, we did it. Now how are we going to make Mom and Dad let us keep them?" As they walked down the road to the cabin, Dani came up with a plan. "We will keep them wrapped up in our jackets and head straight upstairs to the bedroom."

They managed to get up to her room unobserved, but the

kittens were starting to squirm and complain. "We have to feed them," Peter said. He was starving too.

"I think they eat milk. I'll go down and get a glass. You stay here and watch them." Dani glanced down as she headed to the door. "Ick! One pooped." She picked it up with a tissue and flushed it on her way to the kitchen. Dani came back with a bowl and a glass of milk, but the kittens just ignored it. "Why don't we put some on our finger and drip it in their mouth."

She tired it and jerked her hand back. "Ouch! He bit me!" She pinched her finger. "Look, I'm bleeding."

Peter picked up the offending kitten and put him on the bed. Both of the kittens immediately started yowling. Dani picked up her kitten and wrapped it back up in the jacket and started bouncing and humming a lullaby. Peter did the same with his kitten.

They were both bouncing and humming when the door opened, and there stood the Dugans with amazed looks on their faces. After a minute of stunned silence, they burst out laughing.

"Where did you get these little fellas?" Mary reached out her hands and took the one Dani was holding but the scruff on the back of his neck. "Here, let me see him. Oh, he is just adorable. Ooh, sharp teeth however."

Peter kept bouncing and cuddling the one he had, and Henry came over and petted its head. Peter offered him the kitten, but Henry shook his head. "You're doing a good job there, Peter. You keep him. So, tell us how this happened."

They described the whole experience, and Henry explained that those men were poaching—illegally hunting.

Dani and Peter came downstairs to sit on the sofa and hold their kittens while Henry called the Skykomish rangers. They named the kittens Oscar and Louella. Then the rangers arrived with a reporter from the town newspaper.

The rangers asked them a lot of questions, and they gave descriptions of the hunters. Then one of the rangers reached for a kitten. "We will take them to a wildlife shelter where they will be raised until they can go back out into the wild." The rangers each took one kitten by the back of the neck and headed for the door. The kittens started yowling again.

Peter and Dani continued sitting in silence, just taking in everything that had happened. The Dugans didn't say anything to them about their choices that day. It was pretty clear now that they were on their own and were expected to make wise decisions. It was a lot of pressure. That next Saturday, their pictures were on the front page of the Snoqualmie Valley Record.

CHAPTER 7

*A*fter the dinner with Jessica, Peter stopped by the boys club to see James. "How's it going here?"

"Great! I'm glad you stopped by. I haven't had a chance to talk to you since you went to the funeral. How was it seeing Dani again?" James handed Peter a soda.

"She is amazing. She has had a hard time of it, but her spark is still there. I got chewed out for not writing her back." He chuckled. "I know I made the right choice there, but she was not happy about it." He had no idea Dani would become such a beautiful woman.

"You know, James, she is the most beautiful woman I have ever seen, and that is saying something." If James could take the time to talk, he wanted to bounce some ideas off of him.

James was excited. "This is the beginning of a new life for you."

"James, who's to say if she will even be interested in me now? Besides, it's indecent to even try to see her right away."

"It has been several months. Give it some more time, but you could make contact now and then, just to keep your name in the picture. You know, send her a copy of one of those pictures you scoured up from your trip to Washington with her family."

James continued, "Maybe get on her Facebook and email; eventually you could start texting."

"These are all good ideas, James. Thanks."

Peter headed home. It was a long drive, but he appreciated the time to think and unwind in the limo.

Even though there was actually a possibility that they could one day be together, he still felt that nagging voice in his head, *You will ruin her life.* He was afraid to go forward. But he was also so drawn toward her, he didn't know if he could stay away.

He carried the arrowhead and the coin in his pocket. They represented both the joy he had as he thought of being with Dani and the fear of ruining her life. He flipped them over and over in one hand. It had become a nervous habit. The turmoil in his heart was real. He sighed and put them back in his pocket. He was tired and needed to rest his mind.

He took off his shoes and kicked back. He never could look at a pair of shoes without thinking of the Dugan's and Christmas.

Every year they had a couple presents for him under their tree. One was always a pair of new shoes. They always bought the most popular shoes that year for him.

Peter drifted back to the day it all started. He was seven years old. He was in coed gym class and was putting on his gym shoes to play volleyball. One of the kids in the class reached over and grabbed one of his shoes. "Look at Peter's holey shoes. Are you going to be a preacher?" He ran all over the gym, showing everyone his shoe. Everybody laughed except Dani. She turned red as her temper grew hot. When the kid finally came back, she took the shoe out of his hand and hit him over the head with it as hard as she could. He fell down crying, and she was sent to the principal's office. Dani told him later that her parents had to come over to the school and convince the principal she wasn't going to be any further trouble.

The Christmas after he turned seven stood out in his mind. He didn't think much about his parents' finances at that age. He just knew he didn't have the clothes or toys that other children in the neighborhood had.

On Christmas morning, Dani showed up at his door. "Merry Christmas! Mrs. Jacobs, can Peter come over to play?" Before Dani could step in the house, Peter ran to the door to stand in her way. His father had passed out on the living room floor the night before. His mother smiled at Dani and nodded.

"I have a big surprise for you," Dani said. "I picked them out myself." They walked through the mud around the back of her house and came up the back steps. After they came in the back door, they sat down and took off their shoes. In stocking feet, they padded through the kitchen.

Dani's mother was busy cooking and looked up with a smile when she saw them. "Merry Christmas, Peter! How are your parents doing this morning?"

"Merry Christmas, ma'am. They are okay; Dad is still sleeping."

"I am going to give them a call a little later today. Why don't you and Dani go see what's under the Christmas tree?"

The kitchen was painted a cheery yellow with white trim. There was a cookie jar that looked like a big red apple sitting on the counter, which always seemed to have cookies inside. The kitchen window was over the sink and had colorful curtains with pink and yellow flowers. The pantry door was open, and

Peter was amazed to see how much food was in there. The top two shelves were full of jars of peaches, pears, and tomatoes. The lower shelves were full of canned goods of every kind: soups, beans, peas, corn, beets, pineapple and little jars of jelly. Sometimes at his house, there was nothing but soda crackers to eat. The Dugans would never go hungry.

As they opened the door to the living room, the strong scent of pine filled his nostrils. Dani ran over to the tree and picked up a clumsily wrapped box and handed it to Peter. "Sit down and open this. I'm so excited."

Peter was nervous opening the box, trying to save the beautiful paper. Finally Dani started tearing the paper off to help him. When she opened the lid and he saw the shoes, he just stared and couldn't say a word. They were the coolest and most expensive shoes you could buy.

"Well, put them on!" Between him and Dani, he got the shoes on. They were wonderful. He walked around feeling a bounce to his step. He'd had no idea what a good shoe felt like.

"We have to go run, Dani."

She squealed her approval and got her jacket. "Mom, we are taking a test run! Be right back."

Dani ran as fast as she could to keep up with Peter. He smiled—he had never felt so good.

That was the end of anyone teasing him about his shoes. From that year on, the Dugans made a point of buying him the best, most expensive tennis shoes on the market for Christmas.

He pulled himself out of his reverie as the limo came to a stop at his front door. His aunt would ask him about his business meeting when he saw her. She wanted to know and love her posterity before she left this earth. This woman normally got what she wanted. He'd have breakfast with her and report then. Peter smiled as he went up to his room.

He changed his clothes and sat in his office. Peter leaned back and wondered how he could contact Dani without breaking any social mores. It made him happy to think of her living with her parents on the Texas ranch they owned. Sam would love being on the ranch, and Henry was a perfect father figure. They had a thriving business and were the perfect hosts. From his own experience with the Dugans, he felt sure that everyone who was a guest at the ranch would leave a better person.

But they also had a reputation that worried him. In his later years, Henry had apparently decided he was a good matchmaker. *What if he tries to set Dani up with one of their guests?* Peter's emotions went back and forth. He wanted to spend his life with her. On the other hand, that voice from his youth told him he had to protect her from himself.

CHAPTER 8

*M*onths of healing and love at her parent's house was just what she and Sam needed. One morning, Dani woke up to Sam squealing with delight. She pulled on her bathrobe and wandered out into the kitchen to see what was up.

"Look, Mom, a puppy!" A darling, little, fuzzy puppy was hobbling along the carpet toward her.

She quickly picked it up and walked to the front porch. "Sam, where did you get this puppy?" She didn't want to look at it too closely because she knew she would fall in love with it. As soon as she set it down in the grass, it peed. "Good puppy!"

"Carson said he wanted me to babysit his puppy during the day until he gets bigger."

"Oh, he did, did he?" She would need to have a talk with Carson. The last thing she wanted was puppy messes on her new carpet. And that bear rug was likely to be a prime location. Although now that she thought about it, that was not such a bad idea.

"He's going to grow up to be a cow dog. I am going to help train him. I'm a cowboy now, Mom, and this is one of my first jobs."

Well, that did it. Carson was a smooth operator. How could she deny Sam now? He looked so happy. Psychologically this was a good idea for Sam. It gave him something to care for and train, taking his mind off of how desperately he missed his father.

"Okay, Sam, I guess the first thing we need to teach him is to do his business outside."

Sam ran into his mother's arms. "Yeah! Thank you, Mom."

"You are going to be a great cowboy, Sam. You are already a great son. I love you so much!" She wanted to squeeze him so hard, but he squirmed away and went out in the yard to begin puppy training.

"Have you had breakfast?"

"I ate over at Grandma's." *Well, I did sleep in late.* She knew she would never be the cook that her mother was—that was a given. She had tried, all those years with Mitch. It was just no use. Some people have the knack and some do not.

The phone rang. "Hi, Mom. Yes, I'm fine. I just couldn't get to sleep last night." She kept thinking about Peter and the man he had turned into. There was something reassuring about having made contact with him after all these years. Just knowing he was there gave her peace. All night, she kept seeing him as the young boy she had befriended. She got out her phone and looked at his picture. He still had the same kind eyes, but he had changed in other amazing ways. "Mitch hit the nail on the head," she said to herself as she headed for her morning shower. "Peter has definitely revived."

Once she was dressed, she called Sam in to get his walking

shoes. "Come on, Sam. We have to go walk around so I can show you the safe places on the ranch and where you need to be careful."

"Can I bring the puppy?" Sam was holding the puppy loosely, and it slipped through his arms until he had him around the neck.

"Here, hand me that puppy." She took him and supported his lower body with one hand and balanced his upper body with the other. "This is a better way to hold him so he doesn't slide down and get choked."

She handed the puppy back to Sam. "Now you try it."

He held him up, but the puppy started squirming to get down.

"Okay, set him down to see what he wants." The puppy walked over and did his business. "Now say 'good puppy.'"

Sam stooped down and praised the puppy.

"Okay, let's walk around the lake first. What's this guy's name?"

"Carson said his friend Cooper sent him all the way from Australia on an airplane. He wants to call him Aussie."

"Okay, Aussie, come!"

Dani loved it here. She sighed and breathed in good, fresh, humid air. Dani burst out laughing at her own thoughts. Well she didn't need to get carried away. The humidity was a little hard to get used to.

They headed across the bridge. "Sam, your grandparents made this covered bridge."

He was looking over the edge for fish. Dani sat down for a minute on the bench that extended the full length of the bridge.

This must have been a lot of work. The bridge had white posts supporting a country-blue roof. It was color coordinated with the house and stables. Sam threw a stick over one side and ran to the other to see it float by. Dani took his hand. "I have more to show you, come on."

Along the road, Aussie stopped here and there to sniff but kept pace right behind Sam. Dani was impressed; this little dog looked like he was excited to learn whatever Sam wanted to teach him. "I think Aussie is tired, Sam. Let's rest a while."

When they got to the bench, Dani sat down to enjoy the view while Sam and Aussie checked out the water's edge. She loved the shade the trees provided on this side of the lake.

The river bottom behind her was left wild. The other side of the lake was well manicured forest and pasture.

"Do you want to see the tree fort?" Dani pointed to it, and Sam took off running. She was left to carry Aussie.

Sam is going to have so much fun on this ranch.

She loved watching the horses in the pasture. It had been years since she had ridden, but she had to admit, the horses her parents had recently purchased were pretty tempting. The palomino that was leaning over the white board fencing seemed to be calling to her. She needed to talk to Carson about the puppy, but it would also be fun to have him share the history of each of the horses. *I am going to have fun too.*

She watched Sam jumping up to a knot on the rope swing. He pushed off of the tree, and the swing carried him over the water and back again. She smiled as her mind jumped back to the loggers swing and the hours she and Peter had spent swinging out over the forest. She wasn't sure she would ever allow Sam to try that one.

Sam's scream jerked her back to the present. He had fallen off the rope swing and wasn't moving. Dani started running at the same time one of the guests came running over from the barn.

She got there just as the man was lifting Sam up and sitting him on the tree stump.

"Let me look at that arm, young man." He turned to Dani. "I'm Doctor Ryan, I'm a guest here." He looked to be in his early thirties and was pretty cute. But when he looked up at her and grinned, his eyes went to her cleavage.

Dani raised her hand to adjust her blouse. "Do you think it's broken?" He seemed to know what he was doing, but she would feel much better if she saw some credentials. And after his behavior, he was already on her bad side.

"His shoulder is slightly distended." He pulled Sam's arm straight out and then took a bandana from around his neck and fashioned a little sling. "You may have to wear that for a couple days. Can you do that?"

Through tears, Sam nodded.

"It's probably a good idea to have his arm X-rayed. I don't think it's broken, but you can't know for sure until you do the tests."

"Thank you, I am Dani Woodlock." Dani shook his hand.

"Will I see you and your husband at dinner?"

"No, I'm not a guest. Thanks for helping." Dani was not in the habit of telling strangers her personal business, and she was not at a point where she could even talk about Mitch's death, so she left it at that and took Sam home.

On the way she walked through the ranch house to the kitchen looking for her mom. "Hey, Mom, Sam fell off the rope swing and hurt his arm. I am going to run him over to Doc Beckers."

"Oh, Sam, come over here." Her mom wrapped him up in her arms and her love. "Here, you better eat one of these." She handed him one of her famous cookies, hot out of the oven. Dani smiled. In her mother's mind, cookies solved all problems —particularly her cookies. She might deny it, but every time she saw a problem, she gave a cookie. She loved that about her mom.

"Thanks, Mom. Do you need anything in town while I am out?" She shook her head, no.

As she looked back, her mother had given Peter a cookie every time he came into the house. Back then he was a little boy with a big problem. Her mother had befriended Adelaide, Peter's mother, soon after they moved in. Mary never shared confidences, so Dani didn't really know anything about their situation other than Peter's dad was ill and his mother was very busy and tired. She heard this many times over the years when she had asked to go to Peter's house to play. Eventually she quit asking.

She remembered that when it was canning time, though, Adelaide was there helping, and she always went home with a couple dozen jars of each thing they canned. Consequently, Dani got out of having to help and sadly never learned how to can. She regretted this now, but she was sure she would be conscripted as soon as the harvest was in this year. This time she actually looked forward to helping her mom.

Sitting in the doctor's office gave Dani some time to think. She wondered if Peter needed a cookie anymore. He surely didn't look like it. She gave Sam a National Geographic magazine about alligators. "Here, Sam, read about these. Sometimes they visit the ranch."

"Whoa, really?" He started thumbing through the pages.

As she thought about Peter, she realized seeing him again had changed things. He was different.

Peter was confident, and there seemed to be an inner strength that had been missing completely when he was younger. She was intrigued. What had happened in his life? She'd missed so much of it that he was almost like a totally different person. She was impressed with how he'd dressed at the funeral too. His clothes shouted money, and his hair was a surprise—he wore it in the latest style. A man needed a healthy salon budget to keep a longer style looking that great.

Dani laughed as she pictured his face as a little boy. His dark, curly hair was always sticking out everywhere until his mother gave him his semiannual buzz cut. She had to admit, he was looking really good now. She considered his request that they get together and talk. She wanted to hear about everything.

The nurse came in to announce it was Sam's turn to be seen. "Come on, Sam, all he'll do is take a picture of your arm. No worries."

"Can I bring the magazine with me?"

"Sure."

The doctor came in with a wheelchair. Dani cringed as the last month came crashing in on her.

"Mom, look, it's Dad's chair."

She took a deep breath. "Yes, Sam, Dad had a wheelchair to help him get around when he was sick."

"He would love this alligator magazine." Sam had the magazine opened to a picture of a huge alligator.

The nurse walked over to Sam. "Wow that is a big one."

The doctor turned toward Dani and quietly said, "We were sorry to hear about your loss." Then he turned to Sam. "Now, what do we have here?"

"He fell off a rope swing and hurt his arm." Dani patted Sam's shoulder while the doctor took off the bandana and gave it to Dani.

Sam answered. "I was climbing into my new tree fort!"

The nurse looked down at him. "Well, I wish I had a tree fort."

"Let's get an X-ray of this," the doctor said. "And I think I can do better than this bandana for a sling." He smiled at Sam. "Why don't you hop in that chair, and Nurse Conners will wheel you down to our picture taker."

Dani knew it would take some time to get over the sorrow associated with Mitch's illness and death. Seeing that wheelchair had just caught her off guard. As a mother, she was sad for herself but very sad for Sam. While the nurse had Sam taking an X-ray, the doctor sat down by Dani. "How are you doing, really?"

"I am so busy looking after Sam that I don't really know."

"Spending time out in the country is a great comfort. Your parents will fill in for Mitch with Sam."

"I worry that I won't be able to be both parents to him." Sam seemed fine, he had a lot of distractions at the ranch, but she knew he hadn't really grieved yet. Maybe that was okay for now.

The doctor's visit confirmed the opinion of Dr. Ryan, and they gave Sam a proper sling to wear. She drove over to Dairy Queen for a treat before heading back to the ranch. She realized she was becoming her mother. Treats did not solve problems, but in her case, a Snickers Blizzard did the trick.

CHAPTER 9

hen she got back to her house, her dad was waiting for her. "Hi, Dad, what's up?"

"I am glad to see Sam is fine. I just got this text from Peter. It's a picture that brought back some fun memories, should I forward it to you?"

"Sure, Dad, send it over."

It was the newspaper picture of them sitting on the sofa with Oscar and Luella, the cougar babies.

"I need to show this to Sam and tell him the whole story."

Henry got up off of the porch swing. "Peter has sure turned into a happy, successful adult. I used to be worried about his future. But he definitely made something of himself. You know he never married."

"What are you saying, Dad?" Dani knew her father too well to think it was an innocent remark.

"Oh nothing, dear, I'm just so happy to see him doing well." Henry walked back through the woods to the ranch house.

"Sam, come on in now. The doctor said you should take it easy. You can keep Aussie in the house with you if you keep him in the box."

She changed into her jeans and headed out the door, yelling back. "Take him out for potty breaks, but come right back inside to rest. I am going over to the stables."

Dani sighed in relief as she walked through the woods toward the barn. On the way, she passed Dr. Ryan.

"How's Sam?" he asked.

She reluctantly stopped to answer his question. "His arm is not broken, so we're good." She started to leave.

"I would be happy to take a look at him in a day or two." His eyes wandered the length of her. There it was again—he was checking her out.

"That will not be necessary." *Slime ball.* Dani walked away from the man faster than she had intended.

"Hey, Carson, could I have a word?"

Carson leaned back against the coral fence and gave the slightest nod toward the doctor. "I heard there was trouble following that one."

Dani wasn't interested in Dr. Ryan, but she was curious how Carson knew anything about the man. But when she asked, he just laughed. "I have my ways, Dani girl."

"From your anonymous past, I presume?" she loved this man. His crusty, old smile still charmed the women. She knew he was living incognito himself, but her dad never would answer her questions about it.

"Never you mind about that, Dani. How's Aussie doing?" Carson had a slight smile as if he'd pulled a fast one on her.

She had to laugh. "Yes, Aussie. Well, to tell you the truth, Sam is in heaven about that puppy. And training him will be a good experience for Sam. I am assuming you are going to give him pointers, because I have no clue how to do this. The only dog I ever had ran the whole household."

"That's the plan," Carson said.

"Sam is resting this afternoon. Can I saddle up that Palomino for a ride around the lake? Its doctor's orders."

"I will get her ready for you. Why don't you take a walk through the stables? We have some mighty-fine animals here now."

"Hey, Carson is that quarter horse in the back ready to foal? She looks big enough for twins." Dani laughed and whistled as she took in the new horses her parents had acquired. These were not riding ranch nags.

Carson nodded. "Your dad wants to give the foal to Sam. He will need to be here for the birth, though. It will help him in the training process."

"Wow, there is a lot of training going on around here. I am going to have to start pitching in." Dani looked in each of the very clean stalls. This was not a simple family operation going on here. This was professional.

"Okay, here you go." Carson handed Dani the reigns. "She's a bit flighty but obeys with a firm hand." Carson helped her up into the saddle.

"We should get along just fine. I am feeling a bit flighty myself."

Dani walked her horse over the bridge and then let her go at her own speed. Carson was right, she took off at a full gallop. The pure joy of it was overpowering. Dani felt such freedom; freedom from the sorrow and freedom from the worry. It all just drained away. About halfway around the lake, her horse slowed down to a walk. It seemed she had some issues to deal with as well. Dani reached down and patted her neck. "Good girl, we needed that."

As she came around the corner, Dr. Ryan was there on the trail. The pure joy she felt soured into an expression that any other man would have read as "go away."

"That was a pretty sight," he said.

Dani kept riding and ignored his comment. She wondered what it was that Carson knew about the man.

Peter sat down to dinner with his aunt Meredith. "You know, Peter, I was hoping you would start dating to find the new mistress of this estate."

"Aunt, there is someone I am interested in. I think I have loved her my whole life, and it's only now that I may have a chance to be with her again. So there's no need to worry. I have a plan to make you happy." He smiled, loving this dear aunt.

His aunt smiled. "I know I am pushy, but just once I would like to see a child slide down the banister in the entryway before I die."

"I am working on that, Aunt Meredith." He knew she would love Dani. He had never talked about her, but the two of them had such a similar personality. And that wasn't necessarily a compliment. They were both extremely bossy and sure they were always right. But even those qualities he found endearing. He couldn't count the times his aunt had reminded him of Dani.

He went up to his room and checked his phone. There was a text from Dani. He immediately sat down to read it.

"Hi, Peter, I had almost forgotten Oscar and Luella until I saw the picture and article. Sometimes I wonder what happened to them. It was thoughtful of you to send it. I can't wait to share the story with Sam tonight before bed. He will love it."

James's plan was working. Peter sat back and closed his eyes, remembering the story. He could still feel her snuggled up against him under the tree, sobbing over the death of the mother cougar.

He texted back. "We have some great stories. Sam seems to be the age where he would enjoy them."

DANI SAT in front of her phone, tempted to write more; she hated to put the phone down and lose this connection to Peter. She didn't want to sound too anxious, but a good idea came to her.

"I think a lot of children would love our stories. Maybe we could get together sometime and write a children's book."

Peter replied, "That is a great idea. But you know what kind of a writer I was. That hasn't changed."

That brought Dani back to his writing assignments for English, all of which she helped him with after the first *F*. She had totally forgotten about that. He would write a paper and they would head to the tree fort, where she would make him read it out loud. They then laughed their heads off about how bad it sounded. She would make him start over and dictate her changes. They argued about whether a boy would use this or that phrase or word. "Boys don't say *really*, Dani. Have you ever heard a boy say *really*?"

"No, but I don't know why you have such a problem with it. How would you say 'really hot,' 'really scared,' 'really important'?"

"I don't know, but I am going to check a thesaurus out of the school library. I know there are better words that boys say."

The next week, Peter had written his paper, which they again took to the tree fort. He seemed quite proud of himself. "The teacher was extremely mad, the children were exceedingly scared, and the cat was categorically snotty."

Peter texted again. "But I would love to get together and make the attempt. How's next week?"

Wha—wait a minute? Next week? Her heart picked up. She wasn't sure she could move forward that fast. Yet she had been thinking of him almost every day, so why not get the suspense over with and just see each other?

"Okay, that's great. Any day is fine with me." Dani hesitated to hit the send button. She shook her head and just did it.

Peter was quick in his reply. "I can be there Wednesday and stay till the end of the week if we need that much time."

"If we are serious about doing this, it will take a lot longer than five days. Can you commit to regular weekends until we are finished?" Dani was never one to do things halfway. You either did it or you didn't, you never just played around with an idea. She was either going to spend time with Peter, or she wasn't. She pushed the button firmly.

"Well, I have some flexibility in my work schedule. I think that can be arranged."

She chewed on her lower lip. Flexibility? What was his job, anyway?

"Okay. Mom and Dad will be happy to hear you are coming. They will have a room for you at the ranch resort."

"I am coming with my thesaurus!"

She laughed, and wondered how she would deal with a very grown up and good-looking Peter.

CHAPTER 10

*P*eter sat back in his chair and wondered how this would go. This was it. At the very least, they could remain friends. And Peter thought that would be good too. He could at least see her and have a small part to play in her life. It was better than hiding Christmas presents on the porch and arranging help anonymously. Sam would get to know him, maybe as an uncle. And as he grew up, Peter would be in a position to help him in the business world.

Even as he tried to convince himself that there was nothing to worry about, he knew he was just setting up a safety net if he didn't get what he really wanted—to love and hold Dani for the rest of his life.

He needed to see James.

Peter walked into the boys club that evening.

"Hi, Mr. Jacobs!" said the young man with ear phones, sitting at the reception desk.

"Hey, Billie, how's it going? Have you seen James around?" Peter took off his suit coat and hung it on the coat rack.

"He's in the gym, I think."

Peter rolled up his shirt sleeves as he walked down the hall to the gym. James had wanted a half-court gym, saying a full court would be too expensive. Peter remembered arguing with him about it. Finally, Peter was so frustrated he'd told him the court was a gift and didn't have to come out of his budget. James agreed and had told him many times since how much better a full court was.

Peter walked into the middle of a basketball game. He moved to the side quickly and sat down by James.

"How's it going?"

James didn't look up. His concentration was on the boys.

"Your plan for Dani is working. Texting her. Sending pictures. The problem is what do I do next?"

James stopped and gave him his full attention. "You're kidding. I never thought that would *actually* work." He burst out laughing.

"You can laugh, but I am going to be there for five days, at least, and I have never had to make conversation with anyone for that long, ever."

"If she is how you've described her all these years, you will have trouble getting a word in edgewise." James scratched his chin. "How did this visit get planned?"

Peter showed him the text messages.

"So she initiated getting together? That is encouraging. I think you are home free." James patted him on the back.

"I wish I had your confidence." Peter sighed.

* * *

DANI WANDERED into the kitchen of the main house with Sam.

"Hi, Sam," Mary said. "How's your arm doing today? Do you need another cookie?"

"Yes, Grandma, Mom says I have to go to bed now so my arm can get better. Could I please have a glass of milk too?" Mary pulled out a stool for Sam to sit on. Dani helped him up, being careful of his arm and sat next to him.

"Mom, I texted Peter to thank him for the newspaper article. We exchanged a few texts and the short story is he's coming to visit next Wednesday."

Mary stopped organizing the next day's meals and sat down. "What do you think about this?"

"I have mixed emotions. We got to talking about the fun adventures we had as kids and decided to write them down for a children's book."

"That is a wonderful idea, Dani. I can't tell you how much fun your father and I had over the years, watching you two."

Henry came in for his nightly cookie. Dani wondered how it was that there were so many cookies eaten in this house and no one had the body to show it.

"Dad, Peter is coming for a visit."

"That's nice." Henry took his cookie and walked back out toward the porch.

Dani looked at her Mom and wrinkled her forehead, not quite believing her father's reaction. "Doesn't he like Peter?"

"Oh, don't be ridiculous. He loves Peter, always has." Mary left and walked out to the porch after Henry.

She came back in, a moment later. "Sam, Grandpa wants to talk to you on the porch."

After Sam headed out, Dani looked at her mom. "What is it, Mom?"

"Your father wants to give Sam the new foal we are expecting. It's a big responsibility, but we think it will be good for him to look after it."

"Carson already has him looking after his puppy. I don't think Sam is going to have time to be sad for his dad. He needs to face it sometime. I'm worried he will have a meltdown if he keeps pushing thoughts of his Dad away."

"That's true, but don't you think it would be good to give him some distance before he has to do that?"

Sam came back in, thrilled. "I get a horse, Mom! It's going to be born here, and it's mine."

"That is wonderful. You are becoming a cowboy more and more every day and you're going to need your rest. Let's go to bed."

It was getting dark as they followed the path to her house. Maybe she would ask her dad to put some nightlights out here. It could be a little spooky at night, and she didn't want to accidentally step on a snake. Just then, Dr. Ryan stepped out from behind a tree.

"Oh, you scared me to death! What are you doing back here?" *Speaking of snakes*

He stepped unsteadily towards her. "Sorry, I didn't mean to scare you. I just came back to see how Sam was doing."

Dani backed up a step and put her arm around Sam. "Look, I don't want to be rude, but this part of the ranch is private property."

His mouth flattened into a line. His glazed eyes were drinking her in. When he grabbed her arm, she knew she was in trouble. This man was sick. The fact that Sam was right here didn't seem to bother him in the least.

Then Carson walked out from the woods. "Dani, I came over to fix that faucet you were complaining about." He looked directly at Dr. Ryan. "Sorry, you must be lost." He stepped closer to the man. "It's dangerous back here. You never know what could happen to a person if he was caught out here wandering around at night."

Dr. Ryan backed away and headed up toward the ranch house, glaring at Carson the whole way. If looks could kill, Carson would be dead.

"Carson, thank you. That man is bad."

"Dani, I think you should sleep in one of the resort's spare rooms tonight. He checks out in the morning. It's either that or I am going to have to sleep on your front porch."

Dani sighed. "Okay. Come on, Sam. Let's go to Grandma's house for a sleepover." Carson walked her back up to the resort and stopped to talk to Henry on the front porch.

At 3 am her mother knocked on her door to wake her up. "Dani, it's time! It's time!"

"For what, Mother?" She groaned as she rolled out of bed. She had been waiting for the day her parents might start to slide mentally. Maybe this was it.

"The foal is coming! Hurry, get Sam up."

Her brain cleared. She put on her bathrobe and went to get Sam. "Sam, wake up. Your baby horse is being born. Quick!"

Sam flew out of bed and ran down the stairs and over to the barn. How did he do that? Only kids could go from a sound sleep to a full sprint in one second.

Dani hurried behind him. All the lights were on in the barn, and the mare was in a larger stall, lying on mounds of hay. Carson and her father were in the stall. Sam was standing in front of Dani, and they all just watched. Dani pulled over a bench and sat down. "Do you need to help her? She seems to be straining."

Carson smiled. "No, this girl knows what she's doing. This is her third foal. Okay, watch this, Sam, here she comes."

The foal's head and front feet came out first. Carson pulled some of the birth sack off of the foal and cleared its nose. A couple more pushes, and the back legs were almost all the way out. Carson again gave them a little pull, and the back legs came out with the rest of the after birth.

Sam looked up at his mother. His face was white. "This is kind of gross, Mom."

Dani laughed. "Yes it is, Sam. But it is also beautiful." Joy and peace settled on everyone. New life came with peace. She looked around at everyone. She could see it on their faces, they all felt it.

The mare stood up, and Carson motioned to Sam to come over. "Now, Sam, pet the foal all over. Just rub gently and talk to him."

Sam tentatively rubbed the foal's back. "Hi, I am your new friend. I am going to call you, Flash. I know you will be fast, so that is a good name. I will take good care of you."

The foal started trying to stand up, and Sam backed away. He looked pretty wobbly, but he made it up.

Dani looked worried. "Carson, the legs are too big. Is that a problem?"

"Well, for a while. He just has to grow into them." He led the foal to his mother's milk. When they left, the foal was nursing hungrily.

Sam yawned as they walked back to the ranch house. Dani held his hand all the way over, thinking of the day he was born.

At their room, they both climbed into Dani's bed and fell soundly asleep.

CHAPTER 11

*T*he days passed as Dani waited for Peter to arrive. She spent her time running to the barn and back, as Sam insisted on staying with Flash. Aussie stood vigil as well. Every chance he got, Sam went in to pet and talk with his new foal. On the third day, they opened the back of the stall to the pasture. Flash followed his mother out and ate his first grass. Carson stayed close by, monitoring to make sure Sam was safe.

On the day Peter was to arrive, her father found her in the barn. "So, Dani, I hear Peter is coming this afternoon. Are you wanting to shower before he gets here?"

"Dad, what in the world?" Dani laughed. "Of course I plan to shower. I have basically been living in the barn the last three days."

"Well, now is a good time. He should be here soon. I'll stay with Sam." Henry put his arms around her. "We love you, Dani, it will be nice to see Peter again."

Dani smiled. "Okay, okay, I can take a hint." She left and walked over to her house. So, her Dad was happy that Peter was coming after all.

Dani was humming a tune as she walked back to her home. After her scare with Dr. Ryan, she was careful to keep her house locked at all times, even when she was home. Dani took a minute to straighten up the living room. Then she went to her closet, looking for something to wear. She settled on jeans and a cute shirt. After showering, she pulled her curly hair back into a ponytail and decided that was good enough.

As she was walking back up the path toward the ranch house, she looked up and saw Peter coming down. She gasped, and her heart started beating erratically. She realized she was scared of what might happen, what she might have started with those text messages. Peter kept coming slowly, looking intently at her with a questioning smile. She relaxed. That tentative smile was one she recognized. *It's just Peter, my friend.*

"Peter, you're here!" She increased her gait toward him, confident now. As she reached him, she took both of his hands. "You're really here."

He smiled, a more relaxed big smile, and they both laughed with relief as the awkward moment passed. "I'm here, ready to work. I think this will be fun," Peter said.

"Well, you know how I love a project. I have notebooks and pens ready for our first workday." Dani took his hand and led him to the ranch house.

"Have you had lunch?" she asked with a wide smile.

Peter stopped and looked at her. "What?"

"I was just thinking, we might not take many breaks...there's at least time for one of my mom's cookies." They both laughed, and the lingering worry and stress melted away.

Dani pulled him in through the backdoor of the ranch house and into the kitchen, where she knew she would find her mother baking cookies for the evening. The smell of the cookies was intoxicating. It brought back memories to all of the guests that graced their halls. The lucky ones remembered cookies their own moms used to bake.

Mary stopped shaping the cookies and took Peter into her arms. "We hope you will enjoy your time here, Peter."

"I've been looking forward to this for a long time." He took a bite. "MMM. I have missed these cookies!" Peter drank the milk Mary had given him.

"Mom, you know Peter is here to work on our book project," Dani interrupted.

"Well, Dani, at least show him around before you crack the whip." Mary laughed and patted Dani on the arm.

"Yes, Mom, of course." Dani got up and headed out of the kitchen and through the lobby. She turned to Peter. "Did you check in yet?"

"Yes, that is all taken care of. Now, let's see this place. I have only seen it in my mind's eye. And where is Sam? I have been anxious to meet him." Peter held the door for Dani as they walked out onto the porch. He stopped and looked at the lake again.

"This place is remarkable, Dani. I can just imagine the adventures we could have cooked up at a place like this." Peter took a deep breath. "Ah, clean country air."

Dani laughed. "Peppered with some horse and cow smell. If you follow your nose, you'll find Sam over with his new colt. He's busy training; we'll stop in later."

Once they reached the covered bridge, they stopped a minute to look over the side into the water. Peter stepped closer, and she felt the warmth between them. "Dani, I've missed you. Those early years were so lonely. Everything that happened I wanted to tell you, to see you, all of it. And then as we both got older, you've just been this amazing memory for me."

She turned to him and stepped into a hug as if it were the most natural thing in the world. Flashes of many other hugs moved through her memory, some wonderful, some painful. Peter put his arms around her waist and pulled her toward him. "Dani, thank you. I need a hug, one friend to another, if that's alright."

Dani looked up at him and agreed. "Sure, I should have hugged you before."

She didn't expect the thrill that surged through her. Peter pulled her closer, and she held him tight and melted into his body. She never wanted to let go.

His hoarse voice whispered, "Oh, Dani." He kissed the top of her head as he pushed back from the embrace.

Dani raised her eyebrows and sighed. That hug had given her something to think about. She loved Mitch, but this felt different. This was a power she had not experienced before. As they walked around the lake, she turned back to study his face.

He raised an eyebrow but didn't say anything.

She just shook her head, confused. If he had feelings for her, why hadn't he answered her letters?

* * *

PETER WAS HAVING a hard time controlling the beating of his heart. He just wanted to grab Dani again and never let go. His dreams of being with her hadn't even come close to what he was feeling now.

Thoughts tumbled through him one after the other. He still had this deep fear for Dani. What if he took up drinking? If he went forward in the face of his genetic flaws but having the strength to give up the love of his life was going to cause some mental battles. In the end maybe they could just be friends. He felt like he was walking a tightrope. Falling off either way was going to be bad.

"Come on, there is a river back here that floods every once in a while. There's fish in this lake, but the fishing is better back there. Do you like to ride horses?" Dani was walking fast and talking faster and leading the way, like always. He had to chuckle. In the beautiful woman walking before him, he could see the little girl with unruly curls falling out everywhere.

The sparkle in her eye showed the excitement she had about their book project. And knowing Dani, they would definitely begin working today. There was no dawdling when there was a goal to accomplish. He had already talked to a friend of his, who happened to be a publisher. He knew she would be on that immediately.

When they reached the far side of the lake, Dani sat on a bench and patted the seat beside her. "Tell me what has happened to you since you left our neighborhood."

"From the beginning?" He felt such love for this woman. To finally be here together—it was a gift. "My mother's sister, Meredith, enrolled me in a military boarding school. I actually liked it and found I could succeed if I applied myself. I graduated with honors and went on to receive an MBA at Harvard."

"Harvard?" Dani spread her arms wide like she used to when

they were kids. "That is amazing! I can't even begin to express how great that is." Dani grabbed his arm and squeezed it.

Peter knew education was a part of Dani's life plan. "Do you plan to continue your schooling?" He thought of her online courses he had paid for.

Her expression was wistful. "Yes, I have always wished I could, actually. I do read a lot, and I'm taking online courses." Dani smiled. "So, what do you do now?"

"I work in New York at a hedge fund. My aunt's been very good to me."

That's great." Dani brushed off her hands and stood back up. "Now, I have everything set up for our first writing session. Let's get to it."

Peter stood up and followed Dani around the lake until she stopped at the big oak tree and pointed up. When he saw the tree fort, he couldn't stop laughing. "We're working in there?"

"What?" Dani asked. "We did our best thinking in the tree fort." But she too burst into laughter as they climbed up the ladder. She had stowed a plastic storage box up there full of paper and pens and some sodas and crackers.

They stayed up in the fort until it started getting dark. Peter was on cloud nine and the sun set way too soon. They talked about their adventures and argued about who said what and when. They laughed as they relived some of the outrageous things they'd done.

Dani said, "I still believe my parents gave us way too much freedom. There is no way I would let Sam do any of this stuff."

Peter nodded in agreement. "We could have been killed on several occasions."

Eventually it was getting too dark to see, and they were forced to climb down. Peter went first and caught Dani in his arms as she came down through the hatch. She turned around to face him, and although Peter was trying to control his emotions, to keep things slow between them, when she stood on tiptoe and reached for his lips he couldn't resist. All the years on the sideline, loving her from far filled him with an urgency that surprised him. "Oh Dani." He mumbled against her mouth and then dipped her to the side, cradling her in his arms, exploring her mouth with his own.

Peter took a breath and sighed but did not let her go. His eyes searched her own, and she stared back full of happiness. He wanted to hold onto this moment as long as he could. He stood her back upright. She smiled shyly and straightened her shirt.

"I think it's time you met Sam. He's probably still at the barn."

He could hear the coin in his pocket clink as he walked next to Dani.

CHAPTER 12

*T*hey walked over to the barn. Dani was worried about how Sam would handle meeting Peter. As they got to the door, Dani took a deep breath and called out, "Sam, are you in there?"

"Over here, Mom. Flash is letting me brush him."

She came around the corner and looked upon the sweetest scene. Flash nuzzled him while he reached to move the brush along his back and down his legs. "Oh, Sam, you are such a good trainer for Flash. You two are going to be great friends."

Sam grinned, face full of pride. When he noticed Peter, his eyes dimmed but he raised his eyebrows in question.

"Oh, Sam, remember my friend who helped me find the baby cougars? Well, this is Peter."

Sam smiled and stood up to walk over and shake his hand. "Wow, that was the coolest story ever."

Relief warmed some of her worry knots. Things just might turn out okay.

Peter pointed towards Flash. "That is one beautiful animal. Can I pet him? How should I do it?"

Sam went over and sat on the hay close to Flash. He motioned for Peter to come join him.

Peter walked over and stooped down to sit by Sam, waiting for his next instructions. "Is this okay? He's a beauty for sure."

Sam took his hand and showed him how to rub Flash's neck. Peter looked up at Dani with misty eyes and a tentative smile.

Dani came over and sat on the other side of Sam. She looked over the top of Sam's head and into Peter's eyes. This was the man she had loved all of her life. This was the man she had chosen at a very young age to be her partner in life, to raise a family with. They had played out this scenario over and over as they grew up.

When Dani looked down at Sam, his eyes were turned up to her, watching, a hint of unease. He looked from Dani to Peter and back.

"So how did Peter do, Sam?"

Sam scowled and stood up. "Dad would have been much better, Mom."

Peter's countenance fell a little. "Thank you, Sam that was really special for me. I am sure your father would have done it much better."

Sam ran out of the barn toward the ranch house. Dani looked over to Peter. "He hasn't had much sleep the last three days since the colt was born. I'm sure he will be okay."

"Don't worry about me. We'll take this at Sam's pace."

Dani stood up. "I will see you tomorrow morning. Thanks for

coming, Peter. I think we made progress on the book." She walked out of the barn to find Sam. He'd picked up on something between her and Peter and it was obviously too soon for Sam to think of any one replacing his father. He hadn't even mourned for his Dad yet she had kept him so busy. What was she thinking starting something up with Peter? She hurried faster. If she knew her mother; he would be eating cookies again. But cookies weren't going to solve this problem.

* * *

PETER WONDERED if he should just leave. Upsetting Sam was the last thing he wanted to do. Maybe he was kidding himself. How did he think he could possibly replace a young boy's beloved father? He slowly walked over to the ranch house and up to his room.

He had four calls from New York waiting for him. He sat down at his computer and answered the calls one by one. But his mind troubled and mulled over Sam's first reaction to him.

That night he slept fitfully. He dreamed that he saw Dani in his mother's ratty chair and little Sam kneeling on the floor beside her crying. He woke up sweating profusely and got up early to shower. He came down to breakfast half ready to check out and leave.

Mary greeted him happily and gave him a flyer. The rodeo's in town today! "Sam has signed up for Mutton Busting, you won't want to miss that." She put some orange juice in front of him . "I'm sure we can get Dani to stop writing her book for an afternoon of rodeo." She laughed.

"I don't know. It might be a hard sell. Mary do you mind my asking; what is mutton busting?" He filled his plate with eggs, bacon and toast and sat down at the big table.

"It's rodeo for kids. They ride sheep. Sam has been practicing at the neighbors with Carson. Dani doesn't know anything about it. He's really excited about the surprise." Mary walked back into the kitchen.

Peter recognized a familiar lack of concern for safety in Mary's plan. He wasn't sure Dani would be too thrilled to have Sam out riding sheep. He was interested however to see how she handled it and decided if he was going to leave, he's go after the Rodeo.

Dani didn't join them for breakfast but found Peter on the front porch later that morning. "Hi Peter, I am sorry I wasn't over sooner. Sam was troubled last night and woke up crying this morning until Carson stopped by and then he jumped out of bed happy as a lark and ran off to the barn. I don't know what to think."

Peter had a good idea but didn't mention it. "I'm so sorry that I upset him last evening. That was the last thing I wanted to happen."

"Oh I know Peter. It was my fault really. I can't be thinking of myself until I know that Sam is going to be okay. You would know better than I how it feels as a young boy to lose your parents."

"Yes," Peter thought back to that day he drove off in the limo. "It was a dark time for me but I do think Sam will adjust. He has your parents and Carson and you to love and support him."

Peter thought maybe Dani really did want him to leave. "Do you think we should put off the book for awhile until you feel better about Sam?"

Dani thought about it. "No I would hate to put off the book, I really think it's going to be great."

Peter laughed. "That was a loaded question of course you would not ever want to put off a project."

Dani laughed. "That's right, I'll watch Sam today and see how he does, then we can talk about it."

Mary came out and gave Dani some tickets to the rodeo. "Carson got us front row seats, I know Sam is excited to go."

"Mom I didn't know anything about this, you know we're working on the book project." Dani got that very familiar look on her face that Peter recognized. Being thwarted. She had a special battle-ready look for the possibility of being thwarted. He had to chuckle.

She turned to him. "What?"

"It's just that thwarted look. I am very familiar with it." Peter kept chuckling as he shook his head.

"Well if we are ever going to get anything accomplished someone has to keep to the project."

"Yes for sure." He wondered if she was going to go into a rant. He watched her, amused.

"Well I am glad you seem to be entertained. But there is no way we are finishing these books in the time we have if we don't get moving on them. I hope I am not going to have to pull you along this whole time." That did it and he broke into hysterics.

Dani blew out air forcefully. "I'm going to get changed. You better too, that is not what you wear to a rodeo."

Peter looked over at Mary with a questioning look.

"Just put on some jeans and a shirt and you'll be fine." She said.

* * *

89

THEY ALL LOADED up into two trucks. Sam went with Carson ,and Dani and Peter sat in the back seat with Mary and Henry in the front. It was just a couple miles down the road; they actually could have walked if they had wanted to take the time.

Dani was sitting right next to Peter and even though she was determined to push aside any feelings she had for Peter until she was sure Sam was okay she couldn't help remembering how safe and peaceful she felt in his arms. But that wasn't all; the thrill of his kiss was something she would not forget for a long time. Her face flushed as she looked over at him.

He reached for her hand, lacing their fingers. What was she going to do about Peter? Sam had to take first priority in her life now. But this physical pull was strong and she didn't want to resist. And the emotional pull was even stronger. Peter felt like her other half.

They drove up and parked. Mary and Henry jumped out of the car saying they would hurry and save their seats. Peter leaned toward Dani and pressed his lips to hers for what might have been a quick kiss, but neither pulled away. Dani clung to him, knowing they might not be free to pursue these feelings.

The announcer's voice blared out through the microphone. They were missing the rodeo. They scrambled out and ran to find their seats, Dani feeling like a teenager, stealing kisses in the back of a truck. But she couldn't regret a single one.

* * *

WHEN THEY GOT to their seats Sam was not there. "Mom where's Sam?"

Henry leaned over. "He wanted to sit with Carson for the first half of the rodeo."

Dani leaned over to Peter. "I hope he's still not upset." She looked at her Mom. "Did he seem upset Mom?"

Mary raised her eye brows and shook her head. "No he seemed very excited actually." They announced the mutton Busting competition.

Dani pointed to the sheep pens. "This is kind of cute Peter, you will enjoy this. I would never let Sam do this but it's fun to watch the young kids try."

Peter eyed Mary who hadn't heard Dani's comment. They announced each child as they tore out of the pen on the back of a sheep, gripping whatever they could to stay on. They each wore a helmet which Peter was grateful for knowing how Dani was going to take this surprise. The riders lasted about 12 seconds each. Then the announcer said, " Sam Woodlock riding the black dragon."

Dani stiffened, her eyes glued to the arena as Sam rode out on a black sheep bucking and bouncing and turning and twisting while her little Sam hung on for dear life. Thirty seconds went by and he was still hanging on. Twice as long as any other contestant. The announcer was screaming into the microphone, a new county record! Rodeo personnel ran out as Sam jumped off. The crowd went wild, everyone standing and cheering.

Dani looked at Peter incredulous, it was the first time he had seen her speechless.

"Your parents have a different definition of safety than we do Dani. We have known this for a long time."

Sam ran up to his mother and jumped into her arms. "Carson and I surprised you Mom and I won!"

Then Sam jumped into Peters arms and gave him a long hug. "Did you see me out there?"

"Yes you were wonderful Sam!" Peter could not help the tears in his eyes. Dani looked over and Peter could see all the anger in her eyes fade away.

"You were wonderful Sam, I was so surprised." She hugged him again. "We should all go get an ice cream after to celebrate."

Carson showed Dani the pictures on his phone. "I will send them over. You have a champion on your hands. A real rodeo cowboy." Carson showed the pictures to Sam. "I will frame the one you choose Sam and we will hang your first place ribbon on it."

Everyone was hungry by the time they got to the ice cream shop so they all ordered hamburgers. By the time they got back home there wasn't much time to write so Dani and Peter took a walk around the lake.

Peter was so happy for the reaction from Sam, for his hug. He could still feel his young and trusting arms around him. He squeezed Dani's hand in his own. "That Sam is a special kid." He wanted to tell her about all the gifts, all the years of getting his Christmas wishes from Santa, about picking out that red bike. He had loved Sam for years now.

"Sam has not really had a chance to mourn for his Dad. I have been worried about that because it's not healthy for him to keep it inside. How can he heal?"

Peter saw that as another road block to their happiness. "Well Dani, if he doesn't deal with it in an open way it could have lasting effects on his decision making and other important aspects of his life." Peter was thinking specifically of his own problems. He reached his hand into his pocket to touch the arrowhead and coin.

"Do you really think so?" Dani seemed even more concerned.

Peter saw the snarling dog in his mind and relived the devastating words that were said. "Even when you know what is right in your life those early years can have a strong hold on your future."

"I would sacrifice my whole life in order to make it possible for Sam to have a good happy life."

Peter knew she meant it. Sam was the all-time project of her life. She was a wonderful mother. His estimation of her rose even higher. She kicked in the dirt. "I don't know how long we are going to be working through things. My parents said you have someone special in New York. I don't know how long it will take to make sure Sam's going to be okay. You should probably move on and find your own happiness."

"Dani there has never been any one for me but you." He put his arms around her shoulder and pulled her close. "Are you cold?" He rubbed her chilled arm and tried to warm her.

"I have to ask, why then didn't you answer my letters?"

Peter knew he should answer or he would never hear the end of it. "The simple answer is I didn't feel worthy of you."

Dani sat straight up, he could see she was in fighting mode now. "That is ridiculous!"

"It may be but that was how I felt." He didn't add that he still worried about his danger to her happiness. He had lived with his aunt long enough now to clearly see what his mother could have become if not for his father. With worries for Sam, and his own concerns that he should stay well enough away drained some of his hope. "Let's get back; it's getting late and you're shivering." He pulled her up and took her in his arms and just held her. She laid her head on his chest, and he wanted to hold her there forever.

"Thank you Peter, thank you for coming."

Peter walked Dani to the ranch house. Sam was wired when they got there, still reliving the mutton busting and probably working off several cookies.

"Come on Sam let's get to bed." Dani hugged her Mom and Dad and said good night to Peter.

Henry said he wanted to walk her down and make sure she was safe.

As she was about to go out the door Dani looked back. "We have to set aside tomorrow for writing."

Peter stood at attention. "Yes Ma'am!"

He heard her say, "Whatever!" and laugh.

Peter slept better that night. It was not the sleep of a happy man it was a sleep of resignation to the possible end of his dreams.

The next morning early there was knocking on his room door. "Are you awake in there Mr. Jacobs?" It was Sam.

"Yes Sam just a minute." Peter grabbed his bathrobe and opened the door. "Good morning. What's up?"

"Mom found out what happened to Oscar and Louelle!" He grabbed Peter's hand and tried to pull him out of the room.

"Wait a second, let me get dressed and I will be right down." Peter quickly got on a shirt and jeans and carried his shoes down the stairs following after. At the bottom of the stairs he stopped to sit and put on his socks and shoes. "Okay where are we going?"

"To my house, come on." Sam took off running. Peter started jogging. It was morning after all and he did enjoy jogging in the mornings. He had to chuckle and hoped Dani was in on this. He followed Sam into the house and into the office where he found Dani sitting in front of the computer.

"Look Peter, it's our kitties."

He squeezed her shoulder in welcome and she placed a hand over the top of his. Two huge cats stared back at Peter from the computer.

She explained that the kitties grew to adulthood at the refuge center. Each time they took them out into the woods to let them go they would find them the next day sleeping on the front porch. They tried taking them farther away and it just took a day longer for them to return.

They became popular with the community and people from all over came to visit the cougars. Soon there was a fund started in behalf of Oscar and Louella and the Seattle zoo agreed to take them in.

Dani clicked on another image. There was a picture of the two grown cougars at the Seattle Zoo. A big sign was in front of their wilderness area that said Oscar and Louella and gave a little history of how they were found and by who. "We're famous! And we can add this to our book."

"Well what do you know. I have thought about those two many times. This is a happy ending to a sad poaching experience."

Peter took a look at Dani in her morning mussed look and loved everything about the thought that he could wake up to this woman. If only. She was wearing pajama bottoms and a t-shirt under her bathrobe. Her hair was a mass of untamed curls sticking out everywhere and her eye makeup was smudged and yet she was the most beautiful woman he had ever seen. The spark in her eyes lit up the whole room with excitement.

She looked up at Peter and pulled her bathrobe closer around her. "I guess we should shower and eat breakfast. Let's work here today. The tree fort is good but getting down is a problem." She gave him a sly smile.

"I was thinking it's the best part about that location." Peter raised his eyebrows and nodded. "But I will be back in about an hour, is that enough time for you?" He turned to leave.

"I'll see you before that; I think we will eat up at the ranch house this morning." Dani got up to turn the printer on. "I want to print this story and the pictures."

"Okay Sam I'll see you at breakfast. Thanks for coming to get me." He winked at Dani and left.

Peter jogged back up to the ranch house just for the exercise of it. He was feeling a little more hope this morning. Sam seemed to be happy and Dani was in project mode and she was always happy when she had a strong purpose to orchestrate.

He jumped into one of the best showers he had ever seen and had to get out much faster than he wanted to. Dani ran a tight ship and he didn't want to be late for breakfast. He had to chuckle this reminded him so much of his Aunt Meredith.

He came down to breakfast to hear Sam talking with Henry about Oscar and Louella. He had brought the pictures with him to show everyone at the breakfast table including the guests. "My Mom is famous, look here is her picture."

Peter joined them and Sam pointed to him. "Here is the little boy in that picture. He's holding the bigger cougar kitty."

Dani came kissed Sam on the head. "What's your plan today little man?"

"I've got chores. Me and Carson are mucking out the stables!" His open grin and fidgety body made Peter wonder if he knew what was in store, but he smiled at the boy's enthusiasm. "Awesome."

Dani watched him run out the door, her expression peaceful. "Let's eat all our meals here today. That way we don't have to stop to fix meals." She passed the fruit to Peter.

"I see we are going to be in project mode today. I'm sure we'll make some progress." He was feeling hopeful that they could make some progress on their future as well. He wondered if she was noticing the happier acceptance Sam seemed to be making toward him.

Peter knew some of his childhood fears about ruining Dani's life were unfounded. He had gone back and forth about this in his mind for months. Nevertheless deep in his heart the possible nightmare still had a strong hold on him. Being here now with Dani gave him hope that everything could be okay. Hopefully they would talk about it today.

"What are you so deep in thought about Peter?" Dani had an annoyed look.

"Oh I'm sorry, my breakfast conversation is lacking I see."

"And you seemed worried. You're so different from the boy I knew, but then sometimes I see him back, like just now. What were you thinking?"

He wiped the concern from his face. "I was just wondering how is it that the remarkable Dani Dugan is even giving me the time of day, this sorry, washed up little kid." He tried to tuck one of her curls behind her ear but it bounced back out. His eyes searched her face, drinking in her nose, her freckles, the curl at the top of her lip.

Her eyes lit and she leaned closer until their lips met. He lingered, still amazed that such a thing was possible.

After a moment, she pulled away. "Let's go for a walk."

As they walked back into the woods toward her house Peter waited for Dani to begin the conversation.

"Peter I have always had strong feelings for you until you stopped writing and I convinced myself all we had planned was just childish." Her irritated side eye would have made him laugh but he knew she deserved a solid answer.

He took a breath, fingered the coin in his pocket and then told her about the butcher and all that he said.

"He did not say that! To a young child. Oh, I'd like to go talk to him right now." Her fists clenched, and he was warmed and reminded of all the times she'd come to his defense.

He shook his head."Dani those words rang true to me. You never really had any experience with my father; I kept you away from him." He brushed the hair out of his eyes. "Now that I am with my aunt and can see how my mother could have lived without my father I am fully aware of the damage an alcoholic can do."

He continued. "Sometimes I fear I'm a time bomb that could go off at any time. The genetic research is there."

They both walked the rest of the way in silence. When they got to the porch Dani said. "You are so careful, so good. Do you really think you're going to start drinking?" Her expression was skeptical but he could tell she was considering what he said. "I'll get our materials; let's sit out here for a while, it's such a lovely day."

When she came back out, she sat down on the swing next to Peter. "I think we could conquer any problems. I certainly have a lot of experience with illness in the family. I've become strong Peter."

Peter thought about that. "You've always been strong." The love he felt for Dani over the years was nothing compared to the love he had for her now in person. His dreams had been but a drop in the bucket to the rush of emotion they felt together. He wondered if he could just let go of these worries and make his dream real. "It's not that I don't want to try. I've never wanted anything so much in my life." He gripped her hand in his.

"Good, because I've wanted to do this all morning." She leaned over and pressed her lips to his. Pleased, he responded immediately, wrapping his arms around her as if holding her would never let her leave, would fix all their obstacles and would allow them to always be together. Her response softened and then Dani pulled back. "Okay now let's get to work!"

Peter shook his head and chuckled. "Dani you can't just do that to a man and expect his mind to stay on the work at hand." He got up and walked toward the front door. "Do you have any sodas in the fridge?"

"Sure get me one too please. I don't want to hinder your writing skills, such as they are." She laughed.

Peter was feeling happy and confident. He could see the realization to his dreams actually becoming a possibility. He grabbed a bag of chips as well and came back ready to work.

They took the list they made of all of their experiences and decided which ones would be a fun story for the next book. Dani picked up her phone to check in with Sam. "Hey kiddo I'm going to read the names of some of the stories I told you about, could you tell me which ones you like the best?"

"Mom I'm brushing Flash now. I liked the cougar one the best." Sam had some of his mother's characteristics and one of them was not wanting to be disturbed when a project was going on.

Peter grinned. "Like mother like son."

She waved him quiet. "Were there any others?"

"I thought it was cool the boy was saved from the waterfall. I have to go now mom. I have chores."

"Okay Sam, thank you, I love you." Dani put down the phone. "Well he isn't going to be much help."

They worked through the dinner hour and accomplished a lot. Most of the stories were uploaded into the computer.

* * *

PETER GOT up and stretched as he walked around the porch. He picked up his phone to check calls. "I better make this call. Aunt Meredith says it's an emergency. I sure hope she is okay."

Dani watched his face, a pinch in her heart making it difficult to swallow. "Oh no, hurry Peter call right now."

He stood as he dialed his aunt's number. "Aunt Meredith what is it. I'm sorry I didn't call sooner." Peter's face dropped. He fell back to the porch chair as if his world had just come crashing down upon him.

Dani reached for his hand. He didn't look up but gripped her fingers like they were his lifeline. "Okay I'll be home tomorrow." Peter wiped the tears from his eyes and put his phone away. Then his face crumpled.

Alarm growing, she wasn't sure what to do for him. "Peter what is it?" Tears welled in her eyes.

"James, my driver and pilot for many years has been in a horrible car accident. He and his son were killed."

He dropped his head, hands clutching at his hair. "He'd been drinking." His eyes, turned lifeless, distant. "I shouldn't be here. I have to go first thing tomorrow morning."

A jolt of fear ran through her. He was talking like this was the end.

"Well, okay. You'll be back though, right?"

Peter took a deep breath and regained some of his composure. "Of course, how else will I keep the story straight?" He laughed halfheartedly.

She recognized his efforts to lighten things up, but she wasn't fooled. "Whatever, Peter. Your memory is a bit faded. I never forced you to hike down that rockslide. That was *your* idea." The banter seemed to be cheering him up.

"My knee was about to come out of its socket, and you insisted, as you always did, that I go that way." Peter smirked.

"Well, then why didn't you listen to me and head back the way we came when we were hunting for raspberries? We could have avoided that rockslide."

"The bears?" He raised his eyebrows in question.

"Oh, those!" They both laughed, remembering the terror they felt as they ran away from that angry mother bear. Dani knew he had won that argument, and she let him glory in it. "So, when can we have another writing session?"

He avoided her eyes. "I'll let you know once I take a look at my schedule." The joy drained from his face again.

They walked up to the ranch house. Neither Dani or Peter said a word. Dani felt the less they spoke, the better chance there was that he would come back. She could sense him trying to make a decision that might take her out of his life. And she felt powerless against a thick wall of darkness she couldn't understand.

Her mother went over to the barn to get Sam and put him to bed.

There was music playing softly in the lobby. Peter jingled something in his pocket and then stood up.

Henry walked in from the kitchen. "Hello, you two." Henry said. "I am off to bed. It's so nice to have you here, Peter."

Peter took his hand. "Thank you so much, Henry. My whole life I've been thanking the Dugan family for your kindness to me. This is a wonderful home you have. A wonderful family."

Peter helped Dani up from the sofa. "I think we should all get to bed. See you tomorrow." He gave Dani a hug and walked up the stairs to his room.

* * *

PETER WENT to his room and tore into himself. How could he have placed them all in this position, knowing what he did about his potential? He accused himself of taking advantage of Dani's revealed need for him. What was he thinking? A picture of his mother passed before his mind's eye. She was sitting in a ratty, old kick back chair, exhausted from working two jobs and trying to get a moments rest. Her premature grey hair falling out of her carefully styled French twist. Her eyes circled with dark rings, with wrinkles from years of stress and worry. He could never do that to Dani.

He was intelligent enough to realize that even if he had the propensity to become an alcoholic like his father, he'd taken every step he could to avoid that possibility. But at the very center of his core, was that young boy's fear of destroying the person he most loved. That risk had always been there, tormenting him. His father's coin, a constant reminder of the terror he felt for his mother. The terror he must keep from Dani.

James was a good man. A recovered alcoholic. Peter had no idea what had come over him to be drinking again, and driving. Twenty years had gone by without alcohol. It was partly James' strength and continued sobriety that had given Peter hope.

When James stopped to pick up his youngest son no one realized he'd been drinking. He hadn't the strength to manage his condition on his own. No one realized the danger he was to his son until it was too late. He plowed into a semi in oncoming traffic killing them both. What happened? Why did he start?

Peter could make a difficult choice now and never put Dani or Sam in danger.

The next morning, he carried his luggage down to the lobby. Sam was there, waiting for him to appear. "Hi, Peter, do you want to have breakfast with me?"

Peter was caught up short. Sam's wide eyes delayed the plan to sneak out before anyone else would see him. "Sure, Sam, I would love to. What's your favorite breakfast here?"

They both walked into the dining room together, and Peter had to admit the table was spread with some very tantalizing options. He smiled and filled a plate. "You know, when I was a little boy your age, your grandmother made me breakfast all the time. I bet I ate breakfast nearly every day at her house, so I know how good this food is already."

Sam smiled and got a plate and ran over to his favorite. "I love Granny's pancakes the best." He smothered them with raspberry syrup and tons of whipped cream.

Peter came over and took a look at his plate. "That does look very good!" He added pancakes to the pile and decided to mimic Sam.

When Peter's plate was adequately piled with pancakes, syrup, and whipped cream, Sam came over with more whipped cream and said, "No no, you have to put this much cream on there." He added a huge pile of whipped cream on top of the mound that was already there. Peter laughed, a little embarrassed by the amount on his plate. They sat down together to eat.

Dani walked in. "Hey, Sam, I didn't know you were coming over here this morning." She took one look at Peter's plate. "So, I see you are having some pancakes with your whipped cream."

Peter blushed a little. It really was a ridiculous amount of whipped cream. "Sam helped me."

"And blaming a child for your total lack of dietary control." Dani laughed.

He winked at Sam. "I have no defense. We can only feel sorry you have yet to discover the best way to eat pancakes."

Dani sat at their table with a plate of fruit and yogurt. "We've really enjoyed you being here. It's meant a lot. To both of us." Peter looked away from her almost-pleading eyes.

Sam piped up, mouth full of food. "You aren't leaving?"

He swallowed a lump in his throat that he nothing to do with food. "Hey now, I do have to go. But thanks for sharing Flash with me. He's one special horse. And you are one amazing kid." He ruffled his hair, but Sam dipped his head.

His eyes found Dani's and their hurt expression tore at him. "I loved my time here. I know how you hate leaving things unfinished." Trying to lighten things up. "We can finish by email of course."

"And Sam, maybe you will send me pictures?"

Sam nodded with his mouth full, whipping cream on both cheeks. Peter handed him his napkin. He could imagine the joy it would be to help raise such a fine boy. After breakfast, he carried his suitcase to the car and turned to wave. But Dani was right behind him and pushed herself into his arms. He pulled her closer and kissed the top of her head, lingering for a moment longer in the life he knew he could never have.

She pulled away and raised her eyebrows in accusation. Her eyes were full of tears. "Come back, Peter. Whatever this is, it will be okay."

Peter shook his head, his eyes teared as he turned to get into his car. He couldn't wave as he drove down the winding driveway and out of her life amid shouts of "Come back!" from Sam. His eyes checked the rearview mirror, and he choked. Sam had grabbed his red Mongoose bike with the black trim and was tearing down the driveway after, waving goodbye.

CHAPTER 13

*D*ani walked back with Sam. "Let's go see Flash." She could barely choke out the words in a normal voice. But she was hoping to shield Sam from the worry she was feeling. She had once again fallen in love with Peter, but her newfound joy was slipping through her fingers as Peter drove down the driveway and out of her life.

"Mom, do you think he will come back?"

"I don't know Sam, I don't think so." Her lips lowered and quivered. Then she took a deep breath.

When they got to the stables, Carson came out looking concerned. "Hey, Sam, Flash has been looking for you." Sam ran into the stables and Carson sat down at the picnic table under the live oak tree in front of the stables.

Dani walked over and sat across from him. Carson leaned back and took a long look at her. "You okay?"

She put her hands on the table in front of her. "I'll be fine; I have to be, for Sam."

Carson fiddled with his keys, not quite meeting her eyes.

"What is it?"

"Well now, I know the timing isn't great to tell you this, but I've been keeping an eye on that Dr. Ryan and doing a bit more investigating." Carson looked over toward the stables and then patted her hand. This wasn't good. It took a lot to rattle him. "He's a very bad character and has been getting away with some pretty evil behavior."

Dani's anxiety level went up. "Well, he went home, right?"

"Someone who looks like him was spotted a couple towns over." Carson's look was severe and angry. Dani had seen him upset before, but this was not the Carson she knew. She wondered yet again what he'd done before he became ranch manager at the Rio Lago Ranch.

"What should we do?" Dani shivered, thinking of his swaying form, gripping her arm.

"I have some plans. I'm also going to put a man by your home, just in case he tries to come this way." Carson stood to leave. "I have friends who will help if necessary." The look of steel in his otherwise kind eyes assured Dani that he was on it. She knew Carson loved Sam and her family. Some of the tension seeped away.

"Thank you, Carson, I will stay alert and try to be more careful as well." Dani headed toward the ranch house, leaving Sam in the stables for Carson's horse training lessons.

* * *

PETER'S FLIGHT back to the east coast was miserable. He had tasted just how wonderful life could be at last with Dani at his side. He had been vacillating between staying completely away and just going for it, regardless of the danger to Dani. But since James' fall off the wagon that would be impossible. He considered again of just being friends, but what was he going to do if she married again, which was highly likely. Then on top of his concern for Dani, his heart ached at the loss of a friend. James had been almost like another father figure to him from the moment he picked him up at the Dugan's.

Once he got home to Connecticut, he threw himself into his work. At night, he tossed and turned, waking up even more distraught than the day before. This went on for weeks. Instead of getting any better, time away from Dani only made his unhappiness worse. And they hadn't kept up with the stories. They hadn't communicated at all. Peter didn't have it in him, and Dani...he could only guess her reasons, but she hadn't reached out either.

One morning, his aunt requested he join her for breakfast. "Peter, I've been hearing some complaints."

Peter brought himself out of his reverie. "Complaints?"

"Yes, now mind you, I never did have a reputation of being kind or helpful to my employees, so your behavior seems perfectly fine to me and more efficient than normal. But your employees are saying you're being a little, I believe the word they used was, uptight."

Peter thought back over the last couple weeks. He'd been miserable and had not paid much attention to those around him. He'd been too focused on wrestling with his loss of Dani.

"What is bothering you, son?" Aunt Meredith's eyes softened as she reached for his hand.

Her use of the word, son, made his chest tighten with love for this dear woman. "I've been thinking about my mother and how her life turned out compared to the life she could have had." He could not reveal the totality of his feelings.

"I see." Aunt Meredith folded her napkin and set it beside her plate. "Peter, I have a gift for you that I have been saving for Christmas. But I think you need to have it today. Let's have dinner together this evening."

That evening, Peter joined his aunt in the dining room for dinner. "Aunt Meredith, this is a Christmas dinner! What in the world?"

He walked over to the sideboard. The table was full of every kind of delicacy. He particularly loved the pomegranate salad. The goose rice stuffing was wonderful. He wasn't fond of the bean casserole, but his aunt loved it so he ate it each year.

"Peter, you know I'm not confined by conventions or dates. I decided to move Christmas for the purposes of my gift giving this evening." She laughed. "And truly, why must we limit ourselves to these traditional dishes just once per year. I want to enjoy them more often."

Peter smiled. He loved this woman who, in every important way, had become his mother. He felt her love, even though given in a rather independent, reluctant way.

"This is great. I could use a little Christmas spirit in my life right now."

After dinner, his aunt invited him to sit with her on the sofa. "Sit here and I will give you your gifts." His aunt looked excited.

Edgar brought a leather-bound notebook and set it in Peter's lap. His aunt smiled through tears. "Peter, these are all the pictures I have of your mother growing up. I would like to share it with you and answer any questions you might have."

This was the first Peter knew of the existence of these pictures. He was a little afraid of what he might see.

The first picture was of Meredith and his mother as little girls, sitting on a horse. As his aunt turned the pages, she weaved the story of his mother's life from picture to picture. When she was done, he sat silent. "I never really knew my mother. She had so much potential."

"Yes, she did, Peter. And she gave all that to Derrek, who she loved with all her heart. Your father was a kind man. He suffered many things in the war that he would never talk about. Those horrors drove him to drink to help him forget. He was never the same after he came back."

Edgar set another notebook in his lap.

"Peter, these are pictures of your father. He grew up close to us. I have had a time gathering all of these." The first one was of his father and mother in their early teens.

Peter looked at their happy faces. It reminded him so much of Dani and himself at that age. "They were friends as they grew up?"

"Yes, all three of us played together at times. He was always the peacemaker of the group. Derrek was talented and well-educated. My father was planning to hire him into the family business after the war. Your father came back from the war a hero. Here's a picture that shows him with his medals."

Peter took the coin out of his pocket and looked at it thoughtfully. His aunt reached for it. "That is your father's medal for valor Peter. He would never talk about it and became very upset if anyone asked. But his fellow soldiers told my father that they would not be here today if it wasn't for Derrek." She gripped his hand around the coin. "He saved each of their lives, their families."

A medal for valor. The coin that had brought such terror to his heart now represented his father's sacrifice for his country, for his friends. A father whose heart was wounded by the horrors of war.

Page by page, she weaved another story. His tears fell to his chest. Here was the true story of his father. *My father was a good man.*

Aunt Meredith handed him her handkerchief and asked him to come with her. "Edgar, get Clark. We are going for a drive."

They drove down the highway just a few miles and stopped at an elegant cemetery. The grave stones were carved and ornate. He helped his aunt walk over to the graves. She stopped at one of the new ones. There on the grave stone was written "Derrek Jacobs and Adelaide Walker Jacobs. Devoted in life, together in death."

He looked at his aunt in utter disbelief.

"I had them exhumed and brought them back home. I will be buried over there by George."

He kneeled down at his father's grave, traced his parents' names with one finger. His father a hero, his mother, giving all to stand by him as he tried to endure his own trauma. As he fought his own demons of memory. "I'm sorry I didn't understand." He knew it didn't excuse his behavior, but it sure helped him understand better and understanding made all the difference.

They drove home in silence. Peter was thinking of all he had learned from this most dear aunt sitting beside him. He could never repay her for all she had done for him.

"Of all the things you have graciously given me, Aunt, this is the most cherished."

Freedom. The dark veil of unworthiness fell away. What she had given him was his freedom; freedom from the insecurities of his youth. He did not come from trash. He did not inherit a genetic predisposition to alcoholism. There were no road blocks now to his happiness.

"My father is a man I can be proud of. He gave his life for his country." He suffered from the horrors of war at a time when he couldn't get the help he needed. He was self-medicating with the alcohol. If only Post-traumatic stress disorder was understood the way it is now.

His aunt would never fully realize the gift she had bestowed. It was a rebirth for Peter. He could look back on his life and realize he was worthy of life's blessings. "Thank you, dear Aunt."

"Now don't get mushy on me, Peter. Let's get home and have our pie and maybe play a little Parcheesi. It's Christmas!"

"Are you sure? You know how mad you get when I beat you." Peter laughed. He knew these specially scheduled Christmas days with his aunt would be cherished memories throughout his life.

"Not as mad as I will be if I ever catch you trying to let me win."

Peter laughed even harder; it was the carefree laugh of a free man.

That night in his room, he texted Dani. "Hey, Dani, would it be possible to work on the book again this weekend? I know it's short notice, but tomorrow would work great for me."

He set his phone down and went into the living room to put on some music. As he grabbed a glass of milk, wishing he had a good cookie to go with it, he heard his phone beep.

"Sure, Peter, we have been hoping you would get back here soon."

His heart hummed with happiness. "Okay, great, I'll be there about 4 p.m. tomorrow. I'm coming with my thesaurus as usual. Also, I have some photo albums I'd like to share."

"Hmm, sounds great. See you then."

CHAPTER 14

*D*ani grabbed her phone and headed over to the ranch house. Carson had his men setting up a security system that would rival the one at the White House. He told her it would be up and running in three days. She felt safer already. As a young child, she was sometimes scared of dark shadows and a boogie man in the closet. She had talked herself out of those fears but when you come across a real evil intended monster, it changes your perspective about your own safety forever. Having Carson there calmed her fears.

At the ranch house, Dani stopped in the kitchen to talk with her mother. "Peter is coming again tomorrow to do some more work on our book. Is there room at the ranch house?"

Mary put down her mixer and looked at Dani speculatively. "There's room, of course. But what do you think about that?"

"I love him, Mom. I have loved him, in some way, all my life."

Mary came around and put her arms around Dani. "I am so happy for you, Dani. He's a good man. I have always wanted him in our family."

The next day, Dani decided to do the day treatment at the ranch house spa. She scheduled a hair treatment, a facial, and a manicure. She'd been helping Carson the last couple weeks with the chores, and she needed some serious help getting all the dirt out of her pores and out from under her nails. It was a luxury to have a spa day. As she came up the stairs from the spa, Sam came running into the house, yelling, "Mom, Grandma, it's time! The new baby horse is being born!"

"Sam, that is wonderful! I will come over as soon as I shower. Peter is coming back to visit today, too."

"Yay!" His little jump in the air made Dani's heart skip. He shouted while he ran back to the barn, "Everyone is coming to watch, and I get to help; it's my job, Mom. Peter can help too."

"I'm very proud of you, Sam. I'll hurry."

Dani headed out the back door toward her home. She was excited to see Peter again. Sam was settling in so well here on the ranch. She hoped Peter had come to terms with whatever was troubling him. That last time she saw his face he was in agony. She hummed as she walked through the woods. It was quiet. Everyone was over at the ranch, watching a foal be born.

Maybe the book they were writing would become a best seller. She laughed. It was a beautiful day. The sun was shining after a fresh rain, and life was good. Dani walked into her house, taking off her soiled clothing as she went and stepped into the shower. She had just finished washing the treatment out of her hair when she heard the door shut. "Is that you, Sam?" Unease coursed through her. Something felt off.

She put on her bathrobe and stepped out into the bedroom and froze. There stood Dr. Ryan, grinning like a wolf about to take his prey. What could she use as a weapon? The knives were in the kitchen. He was between her and the nightstand, where her revolver was located. In just a few seconds, her life flashed before her. Sam would grow up an orphan. She would never see Peter again.

Ryan started walking toward her, still grinning, his eyes full of lust. She backed away, planning to give him the fight of her life. He lunged toward her, and she kicked him to the side and ran for the door. She made it to the porch, but he came up behind her, taking a handful of her hair. She screamed as he yanked her back inside.

* * *

PETER DROVE to the ranch in the truck he'd rented. He figured if he was going to a ranch, he better have a truck. This trip, he brought proper ranch clothing with him and a gift for Sam and Flash.

Mostly he was anxious to share his family albums with Dani. When he got out of the truck, no one was around, so he carried his luggage to the front porch and set it down. He stepped inside. "Is anyone here?" There was no response.

Something about the stillness bothered him. His hair stood on end. "Hello?" Something was wrong, he could feel it. Seriously alarmed now, he walked to the back of the building, wary. A scream tore through the garden in front of him. Dani's scream.

"Dani!" Peter took off running like he never had before. He raced along the path toward the house set back into the trees. He heard Dani scream again. *Please keep her safe.* His heart was in a panic. His breathing came in gasps as he jumped the front steps. His momentum sent him crashing through the front door. A man had Dani pinned in the corner, with his hands around her throat. He turned his head around, snarling as Peter grabbed the back of his shirt and threw him to the floor.

Dani struggled toward the nightstand, gasping for breath. She took out the revolver and fired twice out the door. Then she turned it on her assailant. Peter turned him over and pulled him to his feet. The man looked over at Dani with an insolent smirk. That did it. Peter smashed his fist into his face, effectively wiping that smirk right off and leaving him unconscious.

Peter turned to Dani and pulled her into his arms. In his mind, he was back under the pine tree, comforting her as she sobbed. This time it wasn't a dream.

Carson was first to enter the house with a couple of ranch hands. "Take this piece of trash up to the road and wait there for the police. I don't want him anywhere near my barn or the ranch house. He has defiled it long enough."

Peter helped Dani sit on her bedroom bench. He started to walk away, but she reached up for his hand.

"Peter…"

"I'm not going anywhere, Dani." He settled down next to her.

Henry arrived next and sat down with his arm protectively around her. "Dani. The lines in his face deepened. "We are going to have to do a better job screening our guests. I should have listened to Carson."

"Where's Sam?" The fear in Dani's voice tore through Peter.

"I told Mary to keep Sam at the barn with his foal. He needn't know anything about this."

She fell back against Peter. "Thanks, Dad."

* * *

THE REST OF THAT AFTERNOON, Dani and Peter sat on the bench

swing on her porch. They didn't talk. They both took comfort in the silence.

Mary came down with cookies and dinner. She gave Peter a big hug. "We are so grateful you came. You saved our Dani. Can I get y'all anything?"

"Thank you, ma'am. Could someone bring my briefcase down?"

Mary nodded. "Sure, I'll send the bellhop down right away."

"Mom, how is Sam? Did the new foal get here okay?"

"He is fine, dear. The colt got here faster than we expected, and Sam is still over there with Henry. They'll probably eat dinner there in the stables."

It was hard for Dani to eat, but she took a few bites. After they ate, they moved to the sofa. Dani had stopped shaking and seemed content sitting next to Peter.

Dani looked over at Peter. "I feel safe with you here. It's funny, Peter, all those years, all our time apart, I have always felt you were close, like you had my back."

"Just like you had my back growing up," Peter replied. "You have never been far from my thoughts." He got up and stretched, then looked down at Dani. His heart filled with joy. Here was the woman he had loved his whole life. He would never let her go again.

Dani sat up with a very determined and annoyed look on her face. "You never answered my letters! You shut me out."

Peter brought over his briefcase and then put his arm around her again and pulled her closer to him. He pulled out two beautifully bound, leather photo albums. As he turned the pages, he recreated his life through the lens of these new truths. When he was done, he set them down again and looked over at Dani with a look of tender love.

"Dani, I have loved you all my life. You have never been far from my thoughts or dreams. I cherished your letters, but as I said I didn't feel worthy of your love. Last week, my aunt gave me the history of my parents. I'd always worried that I would turn out to be an alcoholic like my father, but my father's difficulties were not inherited but war given. I was finally free—free to love you."

Dani snuggled closer to him and wiped a tear away from the corner of her eye. "Peter, we could have handled any problem, war given or not."

Mary stopped by then with Sam in tow. Peter stood up to greet him. "Sam, could I have a word with you in the other room?"

Peter and Sam walked to the back of the house to Sam's room. "Wow, this is a great room," Peter said. "You even have your own wooden horse."

"Yep, and now I have real horses to train." Sam climbed up on his horse chair.

"Sam, you are going to grow up to be a wonderful man like your father. I am proud to know you. You know your mom and I have been friends since we were younger than you."

Sam nodded and smiled.

"I love your mom. I was wondering if it would be okay with you if I married her and we became a family.

Sam considered what Peter said. "What about Flash?"

"Flash will be your horse as long as you want him."

"Okay, that is good." Sam gave Peter a hug and ran out and asked his grandma to take him over for night time cookies.

Peter found Dani in her office. "I've asked Sam for permission to marry you."

Dani's eyes lit and then clouded, searching his face.

He took her hand and knelt beside her on the bear rug. He looked down at the snarling bear head. "How appropriate." They both laughed.

"With his permission, I kneel here. Dani, would you do me the honor of being my wife?"

She rested a hand at the side of his face and knelt in front of him, bringing his lips to her own. "Yes, I can't think of anything better." Their kiss was full of promises, of hope and plans for happy things to come. When they at last pulled away, Dani raised an eyebrow, "Finally!"

EPILOGUE

Two years later

*P*eter and Dani were married in the little chapel on the Connecticut estate.

They had a daughter they named Adelaide after the grandmother she would only know from the stories her great-aunt Meredith shared with her.

Sam turned ten and mastered the art of sliding down the mansion's two-story banister without falling off once.

Aunt Meredith spent Sunday afternoons with Dani helping her with her photo book project of Mitch. When they finished, Dani insisted they make another one of Meredith.

They published a new children's book entitled, "The Categorically Exciting Adventures of the Skykomish Forest."

The time for the planned Christmas trip to the ranch resort arrived. Peter had booked the entire resort for their visit. It was

Christmas Eve day. They flew into the nearest airport and hired a limo to drive them the rest of the way to the ranch.

The white board fencing along the winding driveway was decorated with garlands and Christmas lights. The wrap-around porch was adorned with six decorated Christmas trees, and lights shimmered all over the ranch buildings. The pecan trees out front were sparkling with tiny white lights on every branch.

Dani whistled. "Wow, I had no idea my parents made such an elaborate effort to decorate for Christmas."

Peter leaned over to get a better look. "It's beautiful. Look at the lights, Sam."

The car stopped, and Sam leaped out and ran to the stables. "Carson, I'm back!"

Mary and Henry walked out to the front porch as Dani rushed up into the arms of her parents. "This place looks wonderful, Mom. Dad, you look great."

Mary gently cradled Adelaide in her arms as Dani handed her over.

"I hope we arrived early enough to help with Christmas Eve dinner?" Dani looked over to the stables and waved at Carson.

"Well, it was the strangest thing. We came out onto the porch this morning to find three Christmas geese wrapped up and ready to cook." Her mother raised her shoulders in question. "Our staff has had them slow cooking all day."

Dani looked over at Peter. He raised his hands palm up as if he knew nothing about it.

The lobby was beautiful. Four extravagantly decorated Christmas trees graced each corner of the room. But in the small private lounge off to the side, the Dugan's had their own family tree. It was decorated with children-made ornaments from Dani, Peter, and Sam over the years. Strung popcorn made up the garland. Gingerbread men and frosted snowflake sugar cookies hung around simple colored lights. As was their tradition, one gift was opened on Christmas Eve.

Everyone crowded into the room and sat around on the leather sofas surrounding the tree. Sam was excited to show Adelaide the ornaments that he had made and sent to their grandparents. Dani walked over and picked up a large package sitting behind the tree. It was from her parents to Peter. She gently placed it in his lap like she had done so many times before. Peter took his time removing the ribbon and bows and wrapping paper until finally Dani and Sam helped him tear the rest of the paper off and open the box. He leaned back in his chair and smiled as all the Christmases of his youth passed before his eyes. And then he pulled out a brand new pair of Ariat cowboy boots.

* * *

JOIN HERE for all new release announcements, giveaways and the insider scoop of books on sale.

Her Billionaire Royals Series:

The Heir

The Crown

The Duke

The Duke's Brother

The Prince

The American

The Spy

SOPHIA SUMMERS

The Princess

Made in the USA
Columbia, SC
01 September 2022

66429102R00072